The Mamı

The Prequel

By
Kenneth Edward Barnes

This book is dedicated to all those that have an interest in prehistoric life, whether it is human or animal.

Contents

Note to the Reader

The Mammoth Slayer books have been my most popular, and I have over 100 titles.

After writing the first book, I received a Five-star rating and a great review. Since the first positive review, I've had several similar ones. This caused me to write the second and third book in the series. Then, because of the popularity of the first three books, I decided to write one other, a prequel, which goes back twenty-two years before the first story begins. Then, in the late summer of 2020 I began writing what I think will be the last book in the series *The Mammoth Slayers: Rise of the Cro-Magnons.*

The first book in the series is *The Mammoth Slayers*; the second is *The Mammoth Slayers: Last Clan of Neanderthals*; and the third is *The Mammoth Slayers: The Last Neanderthal.* After writing the third book, I wrote this prequel. Finally, I wrote a fifth, *The Mammoth Slayers: Rise of the Cro-Magnons,* which is also the longest.

In September of 2020, I updated this book as well as the other three books in the series. I added a few more words and fleshed out the stories a little bit more. I even corrected a few typos. I've had many great reviews on these books, that is why I wanted to make them even better and as good as possible. I even took the few criticisms I've received and looked to see if I could iron any out possible flaws and make the books more enjoyable, which I believe I have done.

I want to take this opportunity to thank you for reading *The Mammoth Slayers: The Prequel.* I hope you enjoy it. I also hope you will read the four other books in this series if you haven't already. If you enjoy any of them please give an *honest* review. I appreciate all of my readers, especially the ones that enjoy all the work I have put into my books.

Prologue

According to many, the Neanderthals lived from between 100,000 and 35,000 years ago and were replaced by the Cro-Magnon race, later to be replaced by modern humans. No one knows for sure why either of the two prior races died out, or did they? Some believe they are still here because the two races were integrated into modern man or Homo sapiens. That doesn't matter because this is a work of fiction and is *meant to be for entertainment* purposes only.

As I said in the first book, prehistoric birds, animals and people have always fascinated me from the time I first learned of them in school. I would often spend all of my study hall period reading about prehistoric animals, from dinosaurs to wooly mammoths.

Mammoths are still making news because every so often a frozen body of this huge creature is found in Siberia. In the early 1900's, scientists from around the world were served mammoth meat at a dinner from one such frozen specimen. Even today, wolves will eat mammoths if they discover one in the arctic that has been exposed under the thawing ice.

Some scientists believe that the mammoth may soon be resurrected by using DNA from frozen specimens. This would be awesome. Today we only have one living animal from the frozen north that lived during the Ice Age and that is the musk ox. It lived alongside the wooly mammoth, the wooly rhino and other Ice Age animals. Why did the musk ox survive while all the others died out? That is a mystery that may never be solved.

I again want to remind the reader that my books about the Mammoth Slayers are for the reader's entertainment. I have given the characters a personality, a life, and they are just fictional characters that never lived, however, in this story they do. Thank you.

During the first book, Brock is mentioned as the former leader of the small clan of Neanderthals. He had been dead several years when the first story opens. Therefore, we will go back and pick up the story before Brock became clan leader, which was about twenty-two years before the first story began.

Chapter 1

In the Beginning

It is early morning as the hunting party trudges through the knee-deep snow. A strong biting wind is sweeping down from the north and blowing across the frozen tundra. The seven Neanderthal men and their leader, forty-three-year-old Ott, are dressed from head to toe in clothing made from bison and musk oxen skins. The furs are warm but their dress can't keep all the numbing cold from reaching their skin, especially their feet. That is why they can't stop. As long as they keep walking, they stay warm.

Under the men's right arms, they are clutching two flint-tipped spears apiece. The simple spear will be the only weapon they will use to bring down the largest land animal on earth, an animal that can stand 14 feet at the shoulder, weigh over 20 thousand pounds and have tusks 13 feet long.

The men have been tracking a small herd of mammoths all morning. They came across the tracks just after sunrise and have been on their trail ever since. It is not an easy life for any human, but it's the only life they know.

The clan leader, Ott, is a big man as far as Neanderthal men go. Standing at five-feet four inches tall, he's very muscular with broad shoulders and calloused hands. Hands that have held heavy flint tipped spears, stone skinning tools and stone axes. He has deep-set brown eyes under a prominent brow ridge, a rather wide nose, a large jaw and a short neck. His very bushy dark brown beard is sprinkled with some gray as is his long, wavy brown hair and his bushy eyebrows. His body is also covered with black curly hair as are all Neanderthal men. He may look more like a beast than a human, but he's smart. He must be, not only to keep peace and unity in his clan, but to use his wisdom and knowledge to keep them alive and safe during the very long cold winters. A clan leader needs to know how to lead his men on dangerous hunts, when and where to find game, and to show courage. Ott is fearless and needs to be when he faces such dangerous animals as the giant cave bear, musk ox, woolly rhino, saber-toothed tiger, and the biggest and most dangerous of all, the woolly mammoth.

Ott has just reached his forty-third year when our story begins, but that is more than middle age for a Neanderthal man. Life expectancy in this harsh and unforgiving environment is not long. Usually men die of disease or accident by the time they are forty or fifty years old. Ott has been the clan leader for the last fifteen years. He took over when his father was killed by a saber-toothed tiger. The big cat had found a bison that Ott's father and his clansmen had killed and the big cat claimed it for its own. When the men tried to drive it away, it attacked. The men threw their spears but the wounded cat managed to keep coming. Before it died of its injuries, it sank its six-inch fangs into the leader's neck.

Ott's clan lives in what one day will be called Europe. Ice covers much of the northern hemisphere and the earth is locked in this frigid state that will last for many thousands of years. There are plenty of animals to hunt; otherwise the Neanderthals could not survive. There are herds of bison, horses, deer, wild boar and wild cattle. There are also wooly rhinos and woolly mammoths that I have already mentioned. There are dangerous predators, too: saber-toothed tigers, dire wolves, cave bears, and timber wolves.

The Neanderthal clan is typical in size. There are eight adult men, their wives and a several children. Ott's son, eighteen-year-old Brock, is about to be "joined" as they call it to a young fifteen-year-old girl named Rena. Brock, like most Neanderthals, is large boned, muscular, with a prominent brow ridge, wide nose, brown eyes, a long bushy beard and long brown hair. Dark thick curly hair covers his chest, back, arms and legs. He's big for a Neanderthal man, standing at five-foot six-inches tall. He's nearly a perfect specimen as male Neanderthal go.

Brock's future wife, Rena, is an attractive Neanderthal woman. Like all women of the time, she goes topless during warm weather. She also has very long curly brown hair that reaches all the way to her hips, a prominent brow ridge, large jaw, a wide nose and short neck. She stands just four-feet nine inches tall, has wide childbearing hips and large full breasts. Brock feels lucky to have such a pretty woman that will be his wife.

Ott no longer has a wife, she died just a year ago of a disease, but he has his two other sons along on the hunt, Crug and Bogg. Crug is twenty-four. He looks a lot like his father but younger. He does have half his left ear missing, but it can rarely be seen because his long thick hair covers it. His ear was bitten off when he had a fight with a man from a different clan three years earlier. Crug has a problem with his temper and it often gets him into trouble. He has a wife named Ni'na. Ni'na is very robust for a woman, with very large breasts and thick legs. She is short, too, at four-feet ten-inches tall, which makes her look even more stout. The couple have a little seven-year-old girl named Ulda and a little five-year-old girl named Ursa. Since Crug is the eldest son of Ott, he assumes he will be the next leader. He may not get his wish, however, if he doesn't learn to control his

emper and rash behavior. Rash behavior that has been a
ment to him in the past.

Ott's other son, Bogg, is twenty-one. He is a short,
stocky man, standing just five-foot tall. His dark brown
beard is long but rather scraggly. On both arms up to the
elbows, he has long ugly scars, which he received from a
saber-toothed cat; one that he speared and approached when
he thought it was dead. Bogg is very meek compared to his
older brother Crug and gets along with everyone. He, too,
has a wife and her name is Trusa. Trusa is a common-
looking woman with rather small breasts, but often a man
must take what he can get when there are few to choose
from. They, however, have just had a son born a month ago
they named Gogg.

Ott has a fifteen-year-old son, too, and his name is
Brant. He is not along on this trip because of his age, the
danger and the cold. He has been on many other hunts,
however. Brant is slender for a Neanderthal and he has
almost no beard, just a few long hairs on his chin. Some
men mature slowly and a few never have a full thick beard
like most other men. Brant is one of them.

There are also some other men in the hunting party.
One is Augg. Augg is twenty-six and has a wife named
O'ma. Augg is an experienced hunter and very proficient
with a spear. He is very muscular with a long torso and
rather short legs. He is extra hairy with dark curly hair
covering his entire body. He is mild-mannered and speaks
softly. His wife, O'ma is small and petite for a Neanderthal.
She, too, is quiet and goes about her daily chores smiling a
lot and talking with the other women.

Nagar is another in the hunting party and is next to the
oldest man in the clan at thirty-two. Nagar is the kind of
man that sort of blends into the background. There is
nothing remarkable about him as he too is rather soft

spoken. He loves to go on hunts and is good at taking game. He has survived many dangerous hunts and this says a lot about his skill with the spear.

Nagar's wife is named Roosa, who is also Augg's sister. Roosa is the oldest woman in the clan and she is the only one that has any knowledge of medicine, which is very limited. Roosa is rather attractive, with long, dark brown wavy hair, curvy hips and large full breasts. Nagar and Roosa have only one child and that is a daughter named Serna, age thirteen.

Serna is just on the cusp of maturity and seems to always be happy. She is very cute with an infectious smile and dark brown eyes. She has a crush on one of the young men in the clan and is looking forward to the day they are joined.

Durock is also along on this trip. He is just twenty-years-old, a brave man and smart enough that he could be the leader. He stands at five-foot two-inches tall, has a big bushy black beard and a deep commanding voice that gets people's attention whenever he speaks. Durock has a pretty wife named Tomah. Tomah is the most attractive woman in the clan and the men always pay attention to her when she walks by. When warm weather comes the men are anxiously waiting for the women to go topless, especially Tomah, as she is very blessed. Durock and Tomah have a two-year-old toddler named Ock. His father loves spoiling him and can hardly wait until Ock is old enough to go on hunts with him.

Lastly, there is Garr. Garr is twenty-nine years old and stands tall at five-foot three-inches. He, like the other men, has a bushy brown beard and long hair. Garr is the most muscular of the men in the clan and is very strong, able to carry a full-grown deer by himself for several miles upon his shoulders. Around the campfire, he loves to tell stories of the hunts he has been on and keeps his audience captivated by his exciting tales.

Garr's wife's name is Soma. Soma is a small rather attractive woman. She loves to talk about as much as her husband and keeps the women entertained as they work or while they are just sitting around. The couple has three children, an eight-year-old boy named Durr and a pair of twins. The twins are a boy and a girl. The eleven-year-old girl is named Sora and the boy is named Graun.

There is one other boy in the clan that is about ready to turn into a man and his name is Dearth. Ott didn't bring him along on this hunting trip because of the danger and because of his age. Dearth is fourteen and an orphan. His father was killed by a mammoth five years earlier and his mother died two years later from an illness. Many believe it was grief from losing her husband that killed her, not an illness. Dearth has been on many hunts in the last year but not when the men hunt mammoths. They want him to get some more experience before hunting the "great beasts" as they call them.

Dearth is young but he already looks much like a man. He is five-foot three-inches tall, has a thick black beard with dark brown eyes that set far back under a protruding brow ridge. He is quick-witted and has an outgoing personality.

There is also a little girl in the clan that is an orphan. She is eleven-year-old Kuma. Kuma's father died during an attack by a wounded woolly rhino. Her mother died a few months later trying to deliver a little girl, which was stillborn.

These are all of the clam members at the present. A disease swept through the clan nearly ten years ago and that's when many of the older members died. Ott, at forty-three, is the oldest member.

The two dozen men and women that make up Ott's clan are all strong and healthy at this point in time. It is just a fact of life that there will be some that will die and others that will be born. The Neanderthals know this and live their lives the best they can. On every hunt they never know if it will be the last time they go out.

The men on the hunt today have been tracking the mammoth herd for several hours when Ott's son, Crug, sees them up ahead. The herd of about a dozen mammoths is just inside a small forest that is next to the tundra. They are feeding on the tree branches and haven't gotten wind of the men yet. There is one massive bull that has tusks at least nine feet long and he is the one that is the closest.

"There," said Crug, pointing to the big brown bull that is nearest them.

Ott turns to the other men and motions for them to close in. The men clutch their spears and crouch down. Sneaking bent over for several yards, they drop down on all fours and start crawling. The snow is up to their chests but they keep going. There is little meat back at their cave and they must make a kill.

When the men are within striking distance for their spears, Ott stands to his feet. The other men do likewise. They stick their second spear into the snow-covered ground, and in unison raise their spears up, draw them back and start walking toward the herd.

No sooner have they began their forward movement, the big bull catches sight of them out the corner of his eye and turns in their direction. He hasn't gotten their scent yet but he knows the danger of humans. Instantly, he raises his trunk, trumpets loudly and flares out his ears.

Ott knows the men must pick one out of the herd and throw their spears before they run off or charge. "Take small cow," he yells, and the men see the cow on the left of the big bull.

The cow is standing broadside to the men as they step forward and with all their strength launch their flint-tipped eight-foot spears. The spears are sailing through the air on their way toward the cow as she takes her trunk from a branch she is feeding on and turns to see what the noise is. That's when all seven spears hit her ribcage and neck. Upon impact, she spins around to face the men. When seeing them, however, she is terrified, turns and runs through the forest. All the commotion causes the others in the herd to flee in panic, except for the big bull. He is enraged at the men who have dared disturb his females and interfere with his mating.

The men see that he means business and they stand still and show no fear. The giant mammoth, however, wants to test their bravery and steps forward, raises his trunk and again trumpets. When the men do not move, the mammoth lowers his head and rushes toward them, determined to drive them away. The huge beast is barreling down on them but they stand their ground and do not move. This unnatural behavior is unsettling for the mammoth. Every animal on earth moves out of the way when a full-grown bull mammoth charges, but when the men stand still, he is the one that is fearful. His eyes seem to be asking, *"Why aren't these tiny creatures afraid and run?"* Somehow, he can sense they are dangerous. He can also smell the blood of the wounded cow that is now about ready to collapse from her injuries.

Breaking off the charge, the bull stops, looks at the men and turns around. Then, with tail raised and ears flared, he takes off running to join the herd. It was a hair-raising experience for the men and their hearts are still pounding in their chests as they let out a sigh of relief. If they would have ran, the bull would have pursued them and crushed them to death.

The hunting party soon finds the cow. She is already dead and the herd has moved on. The men go to work harvesting as much meat as they can carry back to the cave. They will make many trips during the winter to salvage as much meat as possible. It should be enough to get them through the long cold winter. At least the bitter cold weather will keep the meat fresh as long as the scavengers don't eat it all.

Chapter 2

Cave Life

When the men return to the cave they are met by the women, who take the meat they're carrying and lay it on several flat rocks inside the cave. They then go to work cutting it into smaller pieces so it can be roasted. Some of it they cut it into thin strips for jerky.

Everyone is full of joy when they see the men with all the meat. Dearth wanted to go on the hunt but Ott told him he would have to wait. Dearth has gone on hunts for wild boars, deer and even a bison hunt, but not yet for a mammoth. He needs to get a little more experience and some more strength at launching a spear before trying to bring down a mammoth.

When the men return to the cave, Dearth is the first to ask Brock about the hunt. "Was great beast a bull?" he asked, as Brock comes into the cave carrying nearly a hundred-pound hunk of meat.

Brock grins as Dearth takes the meat from off his shoulders and lays it down on a nearby rock. Brock straightens up, arches his back trying to get the kinks out after carrying the heavy burden so far and then turns to Dearth. "No bull, cow," he answered.

Dearth looks a little disappointed.

Brock smiles and says, "Big bull charged us."

This gets Dearth's attention and he grins from ear to ear. "What did bull do?"

Brock begins telling the exciting moments of the hunt from the time they spotted the herd until they found the cow dead. Dearth hangs on every word as he follows Brock to the rear of the cave where they both sit down.

Later that night, after everyone has had their fill of roasted mammoth meat, the men tell the story all over again and act it out as they tell it. Not only do the youngsters enjoy the entertainment, but the women also.

After the telling of the story, the men perform a 'thanksgiving' dance to the Great Spirit for letting them find the mammoth and for bringing all the men back safe without any injuries. Dearth gets to use a short wrist-sized stick to beat a drum made from a hollow log while the men dance around the fire and chant. It is a joyous time for everyone.

Once the dance is over, Brock goes over to where fifteen-year-old Rena is sitting on a bison skin and sits down beside her. The young woman is to be joined to him tomorrow as his wife. The clan has been waiting until the men made a kill for the ceremony could take place. It was like a sign from the Great Spirit that they had His blessing for the union of the couple. They also needed some fresh meat for the ceremony and now they have it.

Brock and Rena couldn't be any happier. They have been waiting for their joining for nearly a year.

Chapter 3

The Joining of Brock

It is difficult for Brock to go to sleep that night. The excitement of the mammoth hunt was once reason. But what made him even more nervous was his joining that was to take place the next day. He has been waiting for his marriage to Rena for what to him seems like an eternity. He doesn't know what to expect when it comes to being with a woman sexually. His older brothers would not tell him very much about it. When he would ask the older men in the clan about sex with a woman, they would just grin and tell him he would know what to do when the time came.

Sex is not something Neanderthals are ashamed of and he knows it is something great and wonderful. He often hears the women moaning and groaning with pleasure during the night when their husbands make love to them. Even before he began changing from a boy to a man, the sounds he heard the women make when having sex would cause him to become aroused. Not only in his body but also in his mind, and he couldn't wait to be a husband and experience it for himself. Tomorrow night, however, he will know first-hand what all the to-do is about.

Sleep finally finds Brock and the next thing he knows it is morning. Upon awaking, the first thing that pops into his mind is that it is his wedding day.

It is barely getting light outside as he looks around the cave and sees that everyone is still asleep. Crawling out from under the bison robe, Brock stands to his feet and looks over to where his future bride is sleeping. All he can see is a large lump under a large bison skin. Quietly, he walks over, kneels down and pulls the robe back to reveal her face. She looks almost angelic as she sleeps.

When Rena feels the cover come off her face, the cool air wakes her. Opening her eyes, she looks up and sees Brock staring down at her with a big smile. She smiles back then turns onto her back, still looking into his face.

"Rena still sleepy?" Brock asked.

Rena blinks trying to get the sleep from her eyes. "No, I awake."

"Rena be joined tonight with Brock. Rena afraid?" he asked.

Rena smiles and shakes her head. "Rena no afraid. Want to be joined to husband."

Brock is still a little apprehensive about his wedding night and wonders why Rena is not. "Rena no afraid to be with man?" he asked.

"No afraid," she replied. "Women tell Rena what to do," she added, with a slight blush.

"Women tell how to be with man?" Brock asked, feeling that he has been short changed by the older men, especially his brothers.

Rena nods with the smile still on her face. She can see Brock's puzzlement that she seems to know more about what will happen than he does. "No worry, Rena help husband."

Now Brock is more than a little angry with the other men. He does not want his new wife to show him how to be a man. His older brothers should have told him what a woman wants and expects but they wanted him to learn the hard way. Looking over at his two brothers that are asleep with their wives, Brock stands to his feet. "Brock be back," he said, as he turns and walks away.

Rena watches as Brock goes over to his shoes and puts them on. He then goes over to the fire that has died down and is nothing but hot coals. Taking his foot, he kicks out two very warm stones near the fire. He continues kicking them over to where his two brothers are asleep. Once he is right beside them, he reaches down, pulls up the hide they are sleeping under and kicks the stones under the covers with them. He then stands back and grins.

It only takes a few seconds before something happens. Crug is the first to feel the hot rock on his hip. Brock cannot see his face but when he feels the hot rock his eyes flash wide open, he lunges forward and throws the cover off. "Ahhh!" he screams, jumping to his feet and grabbing his hip and rubbing it.

His yell wakes everyone in the cave. But before Gogg knows what is going on, he feels the hot stone on his leg and he, too, screams and jumps from under the covers.

Both men are standing there looking around with shock and confusion on their faces. Then, when they see Brock standing there grinning, they know he had something to do with it.

Crug, with an angry frown on his face, looks over at Brock. "What Brock do?"

Brock doesn't answer but just looks at him.

Gogg, still rubbing his burned leg doesn't have a frown but looks puzzled. "Why Brock put hot rock in bed?"

Brock's smile disappears and it is replaced by anger. "Brothers not tell Brock about joining with woman. Women tell Rena about joining. Rena tell Brock she show Brock how to be man with woman. Man no want wife tell him what man need to know."

Crug and Gogg look a little lost for words. They should have told their younger brother things he should know about a woman. He had come to them for advice. Brock's brothers have been married for several years and they have experience as to what a woman wants and needs.

Crug's anger subsides and he comes over to Brock and puts his arm around his shoulder. "Crug know what Brock asked. Come and Crug tell little brother."

Brock nods and the two men walk to the entrance of the cave. There is snow outside, so Crug stops and goes no further. After looking around to make sure no one can hear him, Crug begins telling Brock what to do on his wedding night. Brock is pleased to know what a woman wants and needs, and now he is a lot less afraid that he will not be able to please Rena tonight.

After the talk, Brock goes back to Rena who is still sitting there waiting for him to return. Rena has a big smile on her face. She enjoyed seeing Brock stand up to his older brothers. "What brother say?" she asked.

Brock does not want to tell Rena what the conversation was about even though he knows that she knows. "Brock asked brother about joining ceremony," he answered, with a slight grin. "Crug tell Brock."

Rena nods and asks no more. She does not want Brock to lose his self-confidence.

By now, everyone in the cave is wide-awake and getting up. When Ott learns what Brock did, he grins. He blames the brothers for withholding the information he was asking for, but boys will be boys. Ott himself would have told Brock some of the things he wanted to know, but Brock was slightly ashamed that he didn't already know.

Late that afternoon, everyone is getting ready for the joining ceremony. Ott, as the leader of the clan, will perform the marriage.

For the ceremony, the other women in the clan will use red ocher to paint Rena's face. She will also be wearing a necklace made of bones, small shells of freshwater mussels along with the claws of a bear and a saber-tooth tiger. She will also have on her best robe, which is one made of soft deerskin.

Brock will also be dressed in his finest bison robe and he'll have red ocher on his face, arms and chest. In his right hand, he will have his favorite hunting spear. He will hold the tip into the air and the other end will be placed on the ground. This holding of the spears is symbolic of being able to provide food for his wife and children that will come from the joining.

As the couple stands before Ott, Brock is on the right of Rena. Ott looks at each of them. "Now you will be man and woman together," he said, taking his open hands and entwining his fingers. Then closing his hands together, which symbolizes the joining between the two, he looks at the couple. After this, he reaches over, takes Rena's right hand and places it in Brock's left hand.

Glancing behind him, Ott looks at the oldest woman in the clan, Roosa. She is holding two small pieces of roasted mammoth meat. Stepping forward, she hands one to Ott. Taking the meat, he hands it to Brock and Brock puts between his own lips. Brock then turns his head, looks at Rena and leans forward, so she can take the meat from his mouth.

Leaning toward him, she takes the meat from between Brock's lips and slowly begins chewing it. This means she has accepted Brock as her mate and her provider.

Roosa then hands Ott the second piece of meat and he himself places it between Rena's lips. She leans forward toward Brock; he then takes the meat from between her lips and begins to chew it slowly. This symbolizes that she will help her husband and take care of all his needs.

After this, Ott walks over and picks up a large bison robe. Coming back over to the couple, he wraps it around both of them. Being wrapped together in a cocoon of skin signifies that they are now and will forever be together as a couple.

Once Ott does this, he steps forward and hugs each one. At this, all the other members of the clan begin shouting and dancing around the cave. This is the end of the joining ceremony. The couple is now joined and will be until one of them dies.

Chapter 4

Time Marches On

After Brock and Rena are joined, time seems to fly by. Soon she has a little boy they name Trom. The following year, Rena is pregnant again and a few months later, she has a little girl they name Tuma.

Ock is now five-years old and is running around the cave playing every day. His hair is down to his shoulders and he now has his own spear he uses in make-believe hunts. Every time his father returns from a hunt, he wants to know every detail of what happened. He is a happy little boy and his parents, Durock and Tomah, are pleased that he is such a good child.

Gogg has just turned three and is sometimes a handful for his mother. He is constantly on the move, running here and there, trying to go outside or when he is outside, trying to wander away from the cave and explore. He often plays games with Ock and the two of them bring much entertainment and laughter to everyone.

Fourteen-year-old Graun already has his eye on twelve-year-old Kuma as a future wife. It will be at least a year or two before they are joined. He is maturing fast, however, becoming very muscular and good with a spear. With an already full beard, he looks like a man and Brock has allowed him to go with the men on hunts for some animals, such as bison, but not yet on a mammoth hunt.

Garr and Soma's son, Durr, is now eleven. It will be a few more years before he goes on dangerous hunts or wants to be joined with a woman. Durr is rather slender for a Neanderthal but soon he should start going through puberty and thinking about being joined someday. There are only two potential mates for Durr that are in the clan. One is ten-year-old Ursa. The other is eight-year-old Ulda. It will be a while, however, before either one of them are old enough to be a wife.

Crug and Ni'na, who are the parents of both Ursa and Ulda, now have a one-year-old daughter they named Mursa. It will be a very long time before she is ready to have a husband, but time has a way of passing much too fast and before you know it, the children are adults with children of their own.

No one has died during this time from accident or disease, and everyone seems content and happy, except of course Crug, as he seems to always find something to be angry about. Dearth is turning into a handsome man with his full black beard, dark brown eyes and broad shoulders. He has recently gone on his first mammoth hunt, which was unsuccessful. The mammoths got the hunting party's scent and fled before they could get close enough to spear one. It was an exciting hunt anyway and Dearth's now looking forward to being joined with a girl named Serna. Serna is Nagar's and Roosa's daughter. She is nearing fifteen and Dearth is nearly seventeen, a perfect age for Neanderthals to be joined in marriage. As soon as spring comes, Serna has been promised to Dearth as his wife. Both can hardly wait.

Things in life rarely go smoothly for very long, though, and back during the Ice Age, it was no different. It is late winter and the meat supply is getting low. The men killed two bison and a small mammoth just as winter started, but now all that meat is nearly gone.

Ott is still the leader but he is now forty-six years old and already he is experiencing stiffness in his joints from arthritis. His sons want him to stop going on dangerous hunts but he refuses. They think he might have a death wish since he lost his wife a few years back. Without his wife beside him, Ott seems lost much of the time. He thought about trying to find a new wife, but figured he didn't have that many years left and he wouldn't want to leave a wife behind to grieve for him.

A large mammoth herd had been spotted not far from the cave just the day before. As the men gather up their spears, Crug turns to his father, Ott. "No need for more men on hunt. We be enough," he said, staring into his father's tired eyes.

Ott shakes his head and clinches his jaw in anger. "I go on hunt. Ott still leader of clan. If I want to hunt — I hunt!"

Brock hears the conversation, comes over, picks up his father's two spears and hands them to him. "Here spears, Father. We need all men on hunt."

His father's angry expression fades from his face; he grins and takes them from Brock's hand.

Later that morning, the men find the herd about five miles from the cave. The mammoths are along a small river feeding on some bushes that are growing along the bank. When the herd is first spotted, they are about a quarter of a mile away and the men duck behind the bushes to hide. They will use this natural screen to advance forward to get close enough to kill one of the huge pachyderms.

It takes the hunting party several minutes of stalking to get close. When they stop, they can hear the mammoths making low rumbling sounds as they feed. Ott looks back at the men and points toward the river. Three of the men nod, knowing he means for them to go through the bushes and sneak along the river. This way, the men will have a two-pronged attack on both sides of the bushes when they throw their spears.

About two minutes later, the three men are in position. They all start forward, with one of their spears already at the ready and the other spear tucked under their left arm, ready to drop it to the ground just before launching their weapons. Ott is out front when they come to the end of the bushes. The herd is close, very close. They are actually too close, but they have to take advantage of that fact. They are sure not to miss at this range and Ott hurriedly drops his second spear to the ground, picks out the nearest cow and throws his spear with all his might. As soon as the men see which mammoth he is throwing at, they, too, launch their spears. Ott's spear hits the big cow first, followed in rapid succession by the others. She bellows out in pain and turns to face her assailants.

Since Ott is the nearest, she immediately flares out her ears, raises her tail and trunk, then runs right at him. The big mammoth is only a few yards away when she begins her charge. Ott sees her coming and dives into the bushes beside him. But before he can get out of the path of the angry mammoth, she is already on top of him. Using her head as a battering ram, she drives it down onto the tiny man, crushing him against the ground.

The men see what is happening but they cannot stop her. They run toward the enraged animal shouting and throwing their second spears. When the second group of spears hit her, she abruptly stops her rampage, turns and runs to join the others in the herd that have already fled the scene.

Brock is the first to reach Ott, who is curled up into a ball as he was trying to protect himself. The cow had small tusks but she crushed his ribcage with her head and upper trunk. He knows he has several broken ribs and thinks he might have internal damage, which is not good.

As he is lying there thinking about how bad he might be hurt, he hears Brock's voice, "Father — live?"

Ott turns his head slightly, looking up at Brock's worried face and grunts slightly to let him know he is still alive, but badly hurt.

By now, Dearth is standing next to Brock. "Will Father live?" he whispers.

"Not know. Hurt bad," he answers. Brock then looks over at the others and tells them to hurry and make a stretcher so they can carry Ott back home. They don't want to make a travois because dragging Ott would jar and jostle him around, which would cause even more pain.

Dearth and the others rush to the riverbank and begin breaking small willow trees in two for the stretcher. By stripping the green bark from the trees in long thin strips, they will use them to tie it together. It will not be fancy but it will give them some way to lay their injured leader down and carry him back to the cave.

While the men are working on the stretcher, Brock kneels down beside his father, takes off his own bison robe and covers him to keep him warm. Ott looks up and gives a slight grin. Brock can see the terrible pain his father is in and knows he has probably gone on his last hunt.

It takes the men about an hour to build the stretcher and have Ott laid on it. They will come back later and get the mammoth that is surely dead by now. First, they must get Ott home where he will be more comfortable.

Two hours later, they arrive back at the cave. When the men come in carrying the stretcher with Ott on it, the women see him and begin crying. The men carry him near the fire and gently lay him down.

Several of the women are stacking some bison hides beside the stretcher to lay their leader on. As soon as they are finished, the men gingerly lift him and place him on top of the soft hides then cover him with two more of them.

Everyone in the clan is worried and they do not know what to expect. Roosa is the only one that has any medical knowledge and it is very limited. She can treat minor things such as a fever, but Ott has many injures inside and out.

Coming over to his side, Roosa kneels down beside him. "Ott hurt, inside?" she asked.

Ott nods and places his right hand on his ribs. "Ribs broken. Ribs poke through lungs," he replied. He has been spitting up blood since he was attacked and knows his lungs have been punctured. He believes other organs might also be damaged.

"Want to have skin wrapped around ribs?" Roosa asked.

Ott shakes his head. "No help ribs. Ott will die."

Roosa shakes her head. "Ott not die. Ott great leader."

"Ott like all men. All men die. Ott die soon."

Roosa does not know what else to say but gets up with tears in her eyes and walks over to the cave entrance so no one can see her cry.

Brock is soon at his father's side seeing if he is comfortable. Ott doesn't feel like talking so Brock lets him rest. That is the only thing that can help him at this point.

The remainder of the day Ott sleeps. The injuries have caused his body to go into damage repair and his temperature quickly rises as his body tries to heal itself.

Ott also sleeps the night through, although Roosa is there sitting up beside him placing a cool water-soaked skin on his forehead to help keep down the fever.

By the following morning, Ott knows he only has a matter of hours to live. He can feel that his insides are severely damaged, his breathing is shallow and he's coughing up more blood from his punctured lung.

Brock is the first to come over to check on him. Roosa gets up and leaves when she sees Brock coming. As she is walking away, she looks at Brock and shakes her head. She has tears in her eyes and Brock knows his father is not going to make it through another night.

"How Father feel?" Brock asked, as he kneels down beside him.

Ott looks up into his son's worried face. "Ott has felt better," he answers, as he manages a slight smile. He then begins to cough; blood comes up and he wipes it from his mouth with the corner of the bison robe.

"Father need to rest more," Brock said.

"Get plenty rest when die," Ott replied.

Brock does not know how to answer; he just looks down at his father with sadness.

Ott then reaches up and puts his hand on Brock's shoulder, looks him in the eyes and grins. "Brock will be leader tomorrow."

Brock shakes his head. "Crug oldest son. Crug be leader."

Ott shakes his head. "Brock be leader. That is leader's right. I leader now. I make Brock leader. My word goes."

Brock smiles thinking how much his father must care, about not only him but also the others in the clan to make such a decision. "I be good leader like Father," Brock assures him.

Ott smiles again, takes his necklace from around his neck and lifts it up to Brock. "Take necklace. Put around neck. Get my spear."

Brock takes the necklace and puts it on, then gets up, goes over and gets his father's spear that is leaning against the cave wall. As he is picking it up, his two older brothers see what is happening and come over to their father.

"What Father do?" Crug asked, staring a hole in Brock.

Ott looks over at Brock who is coming back with his spear. "I make Brock leader of clan. You will listen to him."

Anger shows all over Crug's grizzled face. "I the oldest. I be leader!"

"I leader. I chose next leader," Ott said. "I make brother leader of clan. You listen to Brock."

When Brock steps up beside his father and two brothers, Ott looks at all of them. He then looks around at everyone else in the cave. "I Ott, leader of clan. I make Brock leader."

Everyone nods their heads except for Crug and Bogg.

This makes Ott angry and he looks at his two sons with anger of his own. Ott then repeats himself as loudly as he can, "I make Brock leader. You *will* obey him."

The two men look down with sadness on their faces and nod. "We obey father's will," Gogg replied.

Crug does not reply, but walks off with his lower lip stuck out and a frown on his face like a pouty child.

Gogg looks back down at his dying father. "Crug will obey, Father. Will obey Brock."

Ott smiles and nods, knowing Gogg will see to it that his wishes are followed.

Before the day is over, Ott is drawing his last breaths. Everyone is gathered around him and Brock is kneeling beside him holding his hand. Rena is on the other side with her hand gently laid on his chest. She can feel his heart beating beneath the bison cover as she looks into his face. She cannot hide her tears, not only for him, but for her husband. She can see the pain in Brock's eyes as he watches his father slip away into the great unknown.

Ott sees the worry on everyone's faces. "No worry," he said, looking around at everyone. Great Spirit waiting to take Ott to place where warm all season. No ice, no snow. Summer all time."

With that said, he closes his eyes and Rena feels his heart stop beating. She looks over at Brock and shakes her head. "Father gone."

Brock can barely hold back his tears as he stands to his feet. "Father gone," he said, with a hard lump in his throat. "Great leader gone to be with Great Spirit. We have big feast to honor Father, great leader."

Everyone smiles through their tears and starts preparing a big wake for their fallen leader. He will be remembered for all generations.

Chapter 5

Dearth and Serna

After Ott's burial, Brock assumes leadership of the clan. Dearth does not approach Brock about his joining ceremony with Serna, however, until after a full month has passed. He wants Brock to get over the loss of his father before asking him to perform his joining with Serna, but Brock is fully aware that Dearth is anxious to be joined to the young woman. He knew it long before his father was killed.

When the month has passed, Dearth speaks to him about performing the ceremony, Brock smiles and asks, "Would tonight be good?"

Dearth grins, walks over, puts both his hands on Brock's shoulders and looks into his eyes. "Brock be good leader. Wise leader."

Brock smiles back. "Make the preparations," he said, and Dearth hurries to tell Serna that they will be joined before the day is over.

When he tells Serna the good news, she is overjoyed and runs to tell her mother, Roosa. Soon the word is out that there will be a joining and the entire cave is abuzz with the women getting Serna ready.

As the women are busy with the bride, the men are talking with the bridegroom. They begin teasing him about his wedding night, but he takes their joking in stride, knowing it is something that all men in his clan go through just before they are joined.

By late that afternoon all the preparations are finished and the joining ceremony is about ready to commence. Dearth is seventeen and Serna is fifteen. This is not that young for Neanderthal people to marry. Dearth has wanted this day to hurry and arrive for more than three years. Today it is finally happening.

The ceremony will be conducted just before sunset and it is always done the same. The bride will be dressed in her finest, wearing a necklace with red ocher on her face. The groom will likewise have on his best robe of bison skin, deer or some other animal. He will also have red ocher on his face, arms and sometimes other places. He will also have a spear to hold showing that he can provide for his wife.

The ceremony takes only a few minutes and afterward there is shouting and dancing. From this day forward Dearth and Serna will be joined until death takes one of them to that unknown place beyond.

Chapter 6

The Joining Continues

Dearth and Serna are very happy and after they are joined, time seems to just fly by, and the seasons come and go. Time always seems to go much faster when you are enjoying yourself. Nothing major happens for many months and the clan goes on with their day-to-day lives.

Just one year later, Brant is ready to join the love of his life, Sora. Brant is Crug's youngest brother. He is nineteen and has been waiting for Sora since she was thirteen. She is now fifteen and has developed into an attractive woman, with long curly hair half way down her back, curvy hips and ample breasts.

In a Neanderthal clan there are not many choices when it comes to a finding a mate. Once in a while they will be joined with a cousin but usually, they go outside the clan if there are not any men or women available. Since Brant and Sora have liked one another for so long, they wouldn't think of trying to find someone else.

Brock conducts their joining ceremony as he did with Dearth's and Serna's joining and they are soon husband and wife. They hope to have a long and good life together. This is the hope of all Neanderthal couples but in these times, life is very unpredictable.

Lifespans are often not very long. There are no medicines such as antibiotics, no hospitals, doctors, dentists, or even painkillers. When a person gets sick, they either recover or die. When they are injured, they suffer until they heal or death takes them. Sometimes the injuries last a lifetime and leave them crippled. It is a rough life. This is why when things are going well everyone takes advantage of it and enjoys life the best they can.

After Brant and Sora are joined, they are wished well and it is one of the happiest times, not only for the couple, but also for the entire clan.

Chapter 7

The Chance Meeting

Later that same year, when it is early autumn, there is a rendezvous about six days walk from Brock's cave. Nearly every year many of the nearby clans meet to trade and visit, so they can catch up on the news. The men talk about the hunts they have been on, while the women talk about who was joined to whom. It is a time to celebrate, feast and see people other than the same ones in the clan.

At night, the men build several bonfires where they roast meat of all kinds: bison, musk ox, wooly rhinos, cave bears, mammoths and many other birds or animals they can catch or kill.

After they eat their fill, they beat log drums, dance and many of the men reenact their most memorable hunts. Large crowds gather round to watch the sometimes funny but always entertaining performances.

The young boys especially love to watch the men act out the killing of a cave bear or a "great beast", as they call a mammoth. The women and girls are more interested in clothing, and which young men are available as potential husbands. They do, however, often watch the men and laugh at them performing their "great hunts."

While everyone is engaged in conversation or acting out a memorable hunt, some of the very young children are running around looking at everything. From Brock's clan is

year-old Gogg. His father, Bogg, is busy reenacting the
__ .1e participated in when they slew a mammoth last year.
Gogg's mother, Trusa, is busy talking to some other women.

As Gogg's parents are engrossed in what they are
doing, Gogg is running around the camp. When he sees the
head of a saber-toothed tiger lying on a pile of bison hides,
he stops to look at its six-inch long fangs. While he is
standing there studying the huge predator's head, a little
three-year-old girl comes running by. She is not paying
attention to where she is going and bumps into him.

Gogg is surprised when she runs into him and he turns
to look at her. She smiles, then turns and continues running.
Gogg, of course, has never seen her before and he just
stands there watching her as she runs up to her mother, who
is talking with Brock's wife, Rena.

When Rena sees her come running up to her mother,
her mother reaches down, picks her up and holds her in her
arms. The little girl looks over at Rena and grins.

"Who are you?" Rena asked, smiling back at the little
dark-haired girl.

The three-year-old looks up at her and smiles. "Me
Oona," she replied.

"Oona? That good name," Rena said. "You pretty little
girl."

Oona smiles again but seems bashful, turning her head
and hiding her face between her mother's breasts. She then
wants back down. When her mother puts her on the ground,
she takes off running again.

This chance meeting will not be remembered by Gogg,
Oona or anyone else. These two children, however, will
meet again someday when they are adults and much older.
When they do, their lives will be changed forever. But that

is far into the future and that is a story for another time and another place.

These rendezvous usually take place every year. Sometimes, however, when game is scarce or there is trouble or war between the clans, they are not held. This will be the way it is by the time these two children, Gogg and Oona, are grown.

Chapter 8

It is Time!

Shortly after Brant and Sora were joined, she became pregnant. Time went by quickly and now Sora is nearly ready to give birth. Both she and her husband are looking forward to bringing their child into the world. Brant is hoping for a boy. Sora does not care what it is, as long as the baby is strong and healthy. In Neanderthal clans, babies often do not live past their first birthday. It is a harsh environment and without any medical treatments, babies often die from a number of ailments.

It is early morning, on a late winter day, when Sora goes into labor. Everyone is still inside the cave. The children and many of the women are still under their warm bison and musk oxen hides sleeping. Dearth and Ock have tossed several broken branches on the fire and the flames are starting to grow higher. Most of the men are standing near the blazing fire to get warm before going out on a hunt when Sora tells Brant that she is having pains.

When the other men hear this, they decide they do not want to be stuck in a cave listening to a woman scream all day while she's having a baby. "We go on hunt," Brock said, reaching over and picking up his spear that's leaning against the cave wall.

Brant nods but seems a little nervous.

Brock comes over, puts his left hand on Brant's shoulder and looks into his face. "No worry. Sora have strong baby."

Brant gives a slight grin. "Sora strong woman. Have strong baby. If baby boy, be great hunter."

"Be great hunter," Brock assures him.

The men hurry and get their hunting equipment and leave the cave. It is not very cold that day so they even let seven-year-old Ock and five-year-old Gogg tag along. They don't expect to find any game, except for perhaps an arctic hare, they just want to get away from what's going on in the cave. The women and Brant will be there to tend to Sora. Brant doesn't really like being there himself, but he can't miss the birth of his child. He also knows Sora needs him there.

Like all men, Brant paces back and forth, as he is waiting, often going outside in the cold while his wife is in labor. Hour after hour passes and he begins to get worried.

Finally, he comes to the rear of the cave to check on her progress. She is squatting between two large rocks that are about shoulder high, so she can wrap her arms around them. The men put the rocks there just for women who are giving birth. A squatting position is the natural way for a woman to give birth. Gravity helps in delivering it.

When Sora sees Brant coming, she looks at him with her teeth clinched in pain and her hair wet with sweat as another contraction hits. Brant doesn't know what to say, so he just blurts out, "Baby come soon?"

Sora is in too much pain to answer, so she lowers her head and bears with the pain.

Roosa is standing beside her, looks at Brant and sees that he is very nervous. "Baby come soon," she said.

Rena is on one side of Sora, for both women are taking turns wiping the sweat from her face with a cool water-soaked deerskin and to encourage her. When Roosa tells Brant it won't be long before the baby is born, Rena looks at him and smiles. "Baby come when baby want to come. Go outside. We call when baby here."

Brant nods, turns around and goes back outside to wait. After another hour of walking just outside the cave entrance, he hears a baby cry. When the sound hits his ears, he stops and then grins. Turning around, he hurries back inside to see if it is a boy or girl.

Upon reaching Sora, she is lying on her back on several soft bison hides holding the baby on her breasts. Brant cannot see the front of the baby because it is face down. All he can see is its naked bottom. "What baby?" he asked, coming over to Sora and kneeling down beside her.

She grins and lifts the baby slightly so he can see its sex.

Brant grins from ear to ear. It is a boy and he couldn't be any happier.

Rena looks at his joyful face and asked, "What name for son?"

Brant and Sora had discussed the names and like all Neanderthals, it is usually the woman that names the daughter and the man that names the son. Brant looks at Rena and then over at Roosa. "His name be Mooth."

The women smile and then look down at the tiny baby that is kicking his right leg as if he is in a hurry to get up and join the others in the clan.

"Son want to get up and walk already," Roosa said. "He strong baby."

Brant smiles.

Sora then reaches over and pulls a soft deerskin over her and the baby. She looks up at Brant and he can see she is exhausted.

"Sleep now," he tells her.

She then closes her eyes and falls off to sleep. It has been a difficult day. It was her first baby and she was somewhat afraid of what might happen. Now it is over and her heart is rejoicing. She has given her husband a son. That is the greatest gift of love a woman can give her man.

Chapter 9

The Accident

After Mooth is born, things go well for the clan. Spring is just around the corner and everyone is looking forward to the warm summer months. Mooth is growing like a weed and love is also in the air between Graun and Kuma.

Graun is not quite seventeen and Kuma has just turned fifteen. The couple has already made their intentions known to the rest of the clan and plan on being joined as soon as winter loses its grip over the land the following spring. Many Neanderthal girls are already women at eleven or twelve, while others do not mature until they are nearly sixteen. Kuma is one that has been slow at maturing. If girls are too young when they become pregnant, they sometimes have a difficult time delivering a baby. Graun does not want to take a chance that something could happen to Kuma, so he will wait until next year to be joined with her.

The short summer soon ends and winter is again upon them. The great herds of bison, reindeer, and elk are migrating south to find warmer weather and better grazing. The musk oxen and woolly rhinos, along with many mammoths stay put and eke out a living on the frozen tundra or at the edge of the great northern forests.

Once the cold winds come down from the north, the rivers will freeze, the snow will begin to fall and the men will start hunting for large game. They will need enough meat to last them through the long winter months. The cold weather will keep the meat frozen until the following spring. They will need to make a small percentage of it into dried jerky and also roast some of it. Most, however, will be stored outside in a pit where the ground stays frozen year-round in the permafrost. After storing the meat, they must cover the pit with skins, along with logs and branches on top, to keep out any predators. That doesn't always work and often wolverines and cave bears will break in and steal their entire meat supply.

The men have wanted cold weather to set in so they can go on their first winter hunt of the season. Graun especially has been anxious to go. He wants to show Kuma that he will be a good provider once they are joined.

Brock decides they should hunt for bison. Large herds have been seen not more than an hour's walk from the cave. This was the case a few days ago just before a big snowstorm moved in. Hopefully, the herd hasn't moved far or left the area.

As the hunting party of ten go out early that morning, there is a stiff wind and it is bitterly cold. It has been snowing for the past three days and the strong north wind has caused the snow to be in tall drifts. The snow has stopped now, but the wind is still blowing it across the open tundra.

The men are dressed in several layers of furs from head to toe. Gloves have not been invented yet but they keep their hands tucked inside the warm outer layer of fur to keep them from getting frostbite. Their spears they hold by tucking them under their arms. On each of their backs, the men have a small bundle of hides tied. These are wolf skins, which they will use to cover themselves so they can sneak up close enough to the bison to spear them.

Bison are not nearly as hard to kill as a woolly rhino or a mammoth. They can still be dangerous, however, especially one that is wounded. The youngest member of the hunting party is Durr at sixteen. This is Durr's first bison hunt. Last winter he wanted to go but Brock wouldn't allow him to accompany them until he grew a little more. Durr is small for his age and Brock didn't want him to get injured or killed.

It takes the men nearly three hours to find the herd because they had moved over the last few days. The sharp eyes of Brock and Graun are the first to spot the heard about a mile away. At this distance, the herd will pay little attention to the men. Only when they get close enough for the bison to recognize them as danger or get their scent will they become alarmed. It is a large herd of perhaps ten thousand animals. A short distance from the main herd is a much smaller group of perhaps fifty animals. These are the ones they will try for.

The hunting party continues walking until they are about two hundred yards away from the edge of the small herd. Brock stops, making sure the bison have not gotten wind of them. He then turns to the men. "Put on wolf skins," he said.

The men untie the wolf pelts from the man in front of them and then place the skins on their backs. The skin of the wolves' heads is still attached to the rest of the pelts. The men will use them to cover their own head once they are closer. For now, they will walk stooped over until they close the gap a little more.

After sneaking up to within a hundred yards of the nearest bison, they put the wolf skin over their heads and drop down on all fours. To the bison, the men appear to be a pack of wolves sneaking up on them.

The snow is not deep where the men are because the wind has blown much of it away. This is one reason the bison are feeding here. When the men are about fifty yards away, one of the bison sees them and turns around to face what he thinks are several wolves. When he turns to face the predators, he snorts and this causes several of the bison nearby to turn around to see what he is concerned about. Bison often will not run from wolves. They know if they run, they can become separated from the others, then the wolves will attack the individual. As long as they stay together, there is safety in numbers.

The big bull that first saw the men approaching stands still, snorts and begins pawing the frozen ground with his left foot. He is about ready to charge the nearest "wolf", which is Brock. Just before the huge bison charges, Brock jumps to his feet, and pulls back his spear. By the time he has his spear ready to throw, the other men are also on their feet and likewise have their spears at the ready. When Brock throws his heavy flint-tipped spear, the other men throw theirs. All the spears hit the massive bovine and he reels from the impact. This causes him to change his mind about charging and he turns around and runs off. When he tries joining the others in the main herd, they break ranks with him and leave him struggling behind trying to keep up.

The men stand there for a second watching the big bull run with the spears still sticking out of his body. They know he will not get far because several of the spears seemed to have gone deep enough to have punctured his lung. They do want to keep an eye on him, however, for they can never trust that an animal will go down. Sometimes a huge animal such as a bison can run for miles before they succumb to their wounds. They do not want to lose not only the meat but also their spears.

While the men are watching, the wounded bison disappears among a dozen or so others from a smaller group nearby that have come up beside him. Not wanting to lose sight of their quarry, the men take off running to catch up.

Up ahead, there is a small hill and the herd soon disappears behind it. When Graun sees that the hunting party has lost sight of the wounded bison, he heads for the hill. He wants to get to the top. There he will have a high vantage point so he can look out over the tundra and see if he can spot the injured animal.

Brock thinks this is a good idea and he, with the rest of the men, run to catch up to him. By the time the men are only a few feet up the steep hill, Graun is nearing the crest. The men are looking up at the young man rushing to the top when he suddenly disappears.

"Where Graun go?" Dearth asked.

The men are puzzled for a moment, then Brock realizes what must have happen. "Hurry," he said. "Graun fall in hole."

When the men are nearing the summit, they see Graun's tracks in the ankle-deep snow, but a few feet away they end abruptly at a small hole in the snow.

"Careful," Brock said, as he stops and begins inching his way toward the spot where the tracks end.

"Graun down there?" he calls, as he leans over the hole.

"Graun here," came an answer.

Brock sees the top of Graun's head several feet below. That is all that can be seen because he is in snow up to his chin. Brock grins and looks back at the other men. They are all grinning, too.

"What Graun do in hole?" Brock said, teasing.

"Graun wait for men to come. Graun can no climb out."

"Is Graun hurt?" Brock asked.

"Leg hurt little. Graun be better if men get Graun out of hole."

Brock takes off his outer bison robe and using it as a rope, lowers it down to Graun. Dearth and Durock come over on either side of Brock to help. When Graun sees the robe coming down, he reaches up and takes hold of it. A few seconds later, he is out of the hole and lying in the snow on his face. The others in the hunting party are standing all around him with big smiles on their faces.

Graun looks up and sees their grins. "Graun falling in deep hole make good story to tell around fire at night. Make everyone laugh. Graun happy to make others happy," he said, as he struggles to get up.

"Can Graun stand?" Brock asked, reaching down and taking him by the arm.

Graun nods as Brock and Dearth help him to his feet. Once he is standing, he tries taking a step but his ankle gives out and he nearly falls.

"Graun no walk," Brock said.

Dearth looks at the pain in Graun's eyes. "I carry great hunter," Dearth said, laughing. Then turning around, he bends over so Graun can climb on and ride piggyback.

Graun shakes his head. "Graun not ride on Dearth's back. Make travois, pull Graun home."

The men all laugh.

Right then, Bogg happens to look down to where the wounded bison had run and sees the big bull about a hundred yards from the foot of the hill. He is lying on the ground, with bloodstained snow all around his upper body.

He is not moving and is dead. The hunting party will make three travois, one to carry Graun and the other two to carry much of the meat home. It will take a couple more trips to get all the meat to the cave, but there will be plenty of bison steaks and jerky, which will last the clan for several weeks.

Chapter 10

The Joining of Graun and Kuma

Graun hobbles around the cave for a while, and then limps for a few more weeks more before his ankle heals completely. Not being able to go outside for long walks and confined to the cave has not been such a bad thing for him, however, because he has spent the time with Kuma. They have been talking about their upcoming marriage. The long winter seems to pass very slowly for them both until finally the weather breaks and spring is almost here.

Little Mooth is now two-years-old and can walk. He can also say a few words, but he is still nursing. Neanderthal mothers usually nurse their babies for at least two years, some even nursing them for three.

Nothing major has happened over the winter. Graun is now eighteen and Kuma is sixteen. They will be joined next week and everyone is looking forward to the ceremony.

Three days before the joining, Graun and Kuma are getting ready to take a walk. When they come out of the cave, the sun is high in the sky and it is much warmer than Kuma thought it would be. "Sun hot," Kuma said, looking over at Graun.

"Ground soft and trees getting leaves," he said.

"Too hot," Kuma said, turning around and heading back to the cave.

"No take walk?" Graun asked.

"Be back. Change clothes for walk."

Graun stands there waiting for Kuma to return. When she does, he is pleasantly surprised. She has changed her winter clothes for her warm weather ones, and is topless. All winter she has worn her warmer clothes, which covered her breasts. Graun quickly notices that Kuma has developed into a much more bosomy woman than she was when winter began. Her breasts were rather small then, but now they are large, round and this causes Graun to become sexually excited.

When Kuma comes up next to him, he can't help notice her lovely breasts and Kuma notices that he is staring at them. "What Graun look at?" she teasingly asked.

"Kuma much woman," he answered, smiling.

Kuma is pleased that Graun finds her desirable. She had hoped he would be surprised by how much she had filled out over the winter. That was the reason she never let him see her all that time. She was wanting to wait until they were joined, but then it would be dark when he saw her naked and he would not be able to see her in all her glory. This way he can see what he will be getting three days from now.

The couple continues to walk until they are a good distance from the cave when Graun stops. "Why stop?" Kuma asked.

Graun smiles, turns toward her and puts his hands on her shoulders. "Kuma full woman."

Kuma blushes slightly. "Happy that Graun like way Kuma look."

"Graun much like. Want to be joined with Kuma now."

Kuma smiles. "Kuma happy Graun wants."

Graun then moves his hands down to Kuma's breasts.

Kuma looks surprised and quickly reaches up, grabs his hands and takes them away.

Graun's smile instantly fades and is replaced by puzzlement. "Why Kuma take hands away. Kuma said she want be joined?"

Kuma is about to cry and she turns her head away from Graun so he doesn't see and says in a soft tone, "Kuma want Graun after we joined."

Graun steps up behind her. "We be joined in three days. We no have to wait. We can be joined now."

Kuma turns around and looks into Graun's brown eyes and he sees tears flowing down her cheeks. "Kuma no join with Graun now," she said, turning and quickly walking away.

Graun stands there mystified as to what just happen as he watches Kuma leaving. "Kuma!" he calls, but she takes off running.

Graun's heart suddenly feels heavy like a large stone. For several minutes he stands there staring down the path they were on, then he starts walking back to the cave.

When Kuma gets back, nearly everyone is away enjoying the warm spring day. When she enters the cave, Roosa is standing close by and sees her come in. Kuma still has tears in her eyes and when she looks at Roosa, she quickly drops her head so Roosa can't see her face.

Roosa knows something must have happened between her and Graun, for Kuma is always bright and cheerful. She has been exceptionally happy the last few weeks because of her upcoming wedding.

Roosa watches as Kuma goes to the rear of the cave, sits down on a pile of hides then turns and faces the cave wall. Roosa smiles and walks back to her. "What wrong?" Roosa said, sitting down beside her.

Kuma does not even look up at Roosa, but sniffles, then wipes her eyes and nose with her arm. "No talk about."

"Kuma and Graun have cruel words?" Roosa asked.

Kuma turns her head and looks at Roosa. "Graun want to be joined today. Want me to be wife before ceremony."

Roosa smiles and nods her head. "Man have hard time waiting once man know they will be joined to woman. Not bad thing; good thing."

Kuma does not answer but just stares off in the distance.

Roosa sees that she is wearing her summer clothes. She saw her come in and change before her and Graun took their walk. She herself was a young woman once and knows what Kuma was doing.

Roosa, reaching over, takes Kuma's chin in her hand and turns her face toward hers. "Why Kuma change clothes after all winter?"

Kuma pauses for a moment almost afraid to answer. "Kuma want Graun to see how much Kuma has become woman."

"Kuma has become pretty woman. Did Graun like seeing Kuma?"

Kuma nods. Like too much, want to touch."

"Was touch good?"

"Not know. Take Graun's hands away and run home."

Roosa can't help but smile. Young love is so difficult at times. Neither one understands the other at first.

Kuma looks into Roosa's face. "Was wrong for Kuma to run?"

Roosa shakes her head. "Not wrong. Kuma try to be good woman and obey clan rules."

"Graun angry with me," Kuma said, the tears beginning to flow once more. "Not want to join with Kuma now."

"No worry," Roosa assures. "Graun want to join with Kuma. Graun want Kuma much. He always will want Kuma."

Kuma wipes the tears from her eyes with the back of her hands. "Roosa think Graun not angry?"

Roosa shakes her head. "Man get angry sometimes. Man is man. Kuma make Graun wait and Graun not understand. Think Kuma not want him for husband."

"No, Kuma want Graun much for husband; love Graun."

"Kuma be much happy with Graun after joined. Kuma love when Graun want to touch and be joined with woman. Make Kuma happy," Roosa said.

"No think Graun hate Kuma?"

"Graun not hate Kuma," Roosa answered.

Right then Graun walks into the cave. When he sees Roosa is talking with Kuma he turns to leave. "Graun," Roosa calls. "Come speak with Kuma," and she gets up and leaves the cave.

Graun stands there until Roosa has left, then comes back to Kuma and sits down beside her.

Kuma looks up into Graun's sad eyes. "Do Graun hate Kuma?" she asked.

Graun shakes his head. "Graun no hate Kuma. Want Kuma for wife. Want Kuma till Graun die."

Kuma smiles, leans forward and puts her arms around Graun's neck. "Kuma love Graun. Want to be joined forever."

Graun feels her breasts pressed up against his chest, but he doesn't say anything. He will have plenty of time enjoying her once they are married.

Three days later, they are joined. That night Graun becomes one with his wife and it is the way he has always dreamed of. He cannot see her breasts under the bison robe, but he can see them in his mind because of the sneak peek Kuma gave him and, like her, they are beautiful.

Chapter 11

Thou Shalt Not Steal

Less than a month after Graun and Kuma are joined, an incidence takes place that will change the course for everyone involved. All the men have gone on a hunt and will be gone for at least a day, perhaps two, because the bison herds have moved north to have their calves.

Soon after the men leave the cave, the women and children leave to gather roots, berries and some medicinal plants. Unknown to the women, however, they are being watched.

A strange Neanderthal clan has moved up from the south and they are much more barbaric than those that live close by. This particular clan needs women. No one knows why they have a woman shortage. It could be because of a disease that has killed some of them. It could be just a roll of the dice and many more boys have been born in the clan than girls. Whatever the reason, the men of the clan want two women for wives and they aren't about to ask Brock if there are any available in his clan. They are determined to steal them and make their way south again.

The women of Brock's clan have only gone a short distance from the cave when they come across some plants they want. The plants are near some tall bushes, which are hiding the men that are about to prey upon them. Rena has her two small children with her, six-year-old Trom and four-year-old Tuma. They are playing nearby with some yellow wildflowers they have just found. Seven -year-old Gogg and nine-year-old Ock are playing with some sharpened sticks. They are practicing throwing them, pretending they are hunting. Everyone is in a jovial mood as the women begin working in the warm morning sunshine, gathering the plants and putting them in the skin bags they have brought along.

Thirteen-year-old Ulda is beside twenty-four-year-old Tomah near the bushes. They are laughing and talking, when out of nowhere four men run up behind them. Two men grab Ulda by her arms as two others take hold of Tomah and begin dragging them backwards.

Instantly, the women begin screaming. Ock and Gogg see what is happening and they run to get their sticks they have just thrown. The other women jump to their feet and run to help the women that are being abducted.

By the time the women reach the abductors, Gogg and Ock have arrived and they begin jabbing the strange men with their sharpened sticks. The other women are kicking and biting the strangers at the same time. When Ock's sharpened stick pokes one of the men's ribs, it brings blood and the man lets go of Ulda and grabs the stick. Jerking the stick from Ock's hands, he uses it to strike Ock on the head and then he hits Gogg on the side of his neck. Both boys are knocked to the ground.

A second man then picks up Gogg's spear and begins striking the women that have come against them. Soon both men are hitting the women with the long heavy sticks and they have no choice but to try and get away from these men before being injured.

Once they back off, the two men go back over and help their clansmen take the women. There is little anyone can do but stand and watch as Ulda and Tomah are kidnapped.

As soon as the men are out of hearing, Rena turns to Ock. "Go get the men! Hurry!"

Ock nods and takes off as fast as he can run.

Gogg looks at Rena. "Can Gogg go with Ock?"

"No. Gogg too young. Only slow Ock down. Ock get help. Ulda and Tomah be back soon."

It takes Ock over an hour to catch up to the hunting party.

When the men see him running toward them, they know something is very wrong. Brock turns around and starts walking toward Ock, while the others stay where they are and watch. When Ock gets closer, Brock can see the worry on the boy's face and begins running toward him. As they meet, Ock is so out of breath that he can't speak. Bending forward, he puts his hands on his knees, trying to catch his breath.

"What wrong?" Brock asked.

When the other men see Brock run to meet Ock, they start running toward him, too. Ock would not have run all the way here unless something terrible had happened and the men fear the worst. Someone must have died or was attacked by a dangerous animal. By the time Ock can speak, they have come up beside him.

"What happened?" Dearth asked.

Finally, Ock takes a big breath, looks up at Brock, then at the others. "Men come. Strange men. They take Ulda, Tomah," Ock said, letting out his breath and catching another.

"Men!" Brock said, with surprise. "What men?"

Ock shakes his head. "Not know. New clan Ock never see."

When Durock hears that his wife has been taken, he rushes over to his son, Ock. "Where men take Tomah?"

Ock looks at his father's distraught face. "Men go west from cave."

"Ock, walk to cave and rest," Durock said.

Ock does not answer but gives a slight nod.

Brock then looks around at those in his hunting party. "We go find men," and they all take off running, setting a pace so they can keep going for many miles.

All the way there the men's anger is growing stronger. Durock is more worried about his wife, Tomah, than he is angry. He just wants her back unharmed. He knows that if they can't get her back soon, she will be joined to some strange man and he may never see her again.

Upon arriving back at the cave, the women are outside waiting, still upset and crying. When they see the men coming, they run to meet them.

Rena is the first to reach her husband, Brock. "Men take Tomah and Ulda. We try fight, but they beat us with sticks."

Ock hadn't had the chance to tell the men everything that happened. He was already tired when he found them and now was far behind them on the way back to the cave.

"Many men?" Brock asked.

Rena holds up her hand showing four fingers.

Brock nods and turns to Durock and Dearth. "Get more water, spears and meat. We follow men and find Tomah and Ulda. Men take women all die."

Durock and Dearth, along with the other men, run inside the cave and get everything they will need to track down the men that took their women. As they are gathering up some extra spears, Crug is beside Durock. Durock is joined to Tomah who is Crug's sister. "We find Tomah," Crug said. We kill men and leave bodies to vultures."

Durock looks at him and nods, then they take the spears and head back outside to join the others.

Once everyone is ready, Rena and Roosa lead the men to the spot where the women were taken. A few minutes later they are at the scene of the abduction.

"Here," Rena said, pointing to the drag marks on the ground.

The signs are clear to read. The men can see what happened and the drag marks lead toward the west just as Ock had said. Just then, Ock catches up along with Gogg. Ock had stopped at the cave and Gogg told him the men had gone to the place where the women were taken.

Ock walks up beside his father, Durock. "We fight men," Ock said, pointing at his spear lying on the ground nearby. Durock glances down at it and sees blood on the sharp end then looks at his son. "Ock fight men?"

Ock smiles and nods. "Ock no afraid. Stick man in side. Man bleed."

Durock grins slightly showing his pride in the bravery of his son. "Ock make great hunter. Be great man."

Ock grins at the compliment of his father. Then, thinking this is a good time to ask him if he can go along and help rescue his mother and Ulda, he looks up into his father's face. "Ock go help get mother back?"

Durock shakes his head. "Ock stay. Protect women and children."

Ock is disappointed but he pretty much knew the answer before he asked. His father isn't about to risk his son's life.

Brock and the other men of his clan then start tracking the four men. It is an easy trail to follow, as there are drag marks for a good distance. Suddenly, however, the drag marks disappear. Brock is out front when he sees that the trail is gone. Stopping, he turns to Durock who is right behind him. "Men carry women. No marks."

Durock sees what has happened, too. Now the tracking will be slightly more difficult. The soft earth leaves good tracks, however, especially when there are four men carrying the extra weight of two women.

The men track all that day until night begins to fall. It is getting difficult to see the footprints and they must stop and discus what to do next. Brock thinks he knows pretty much where the tracks are leading. There is a cave about ten miles ahead. He believes that is where they are taking the women. They only have two choices and they talk it over. If they wait until morning to start tracking them again, the men could have the women too far away to ever catch up if they are not at the cave where Brock thinks they are.

Brock decides to head for the cave. Everyone is almost certain the four men would not dare build a fire tonight out in the open. It could be seen for miles. If they reach the cave with the women, however, they could build a fire inside and it could not be seen. Brock also knows dragging and carrying the women that far would be exhausting. The men will be tired and hungry. It also gets chilly at night and a fire would be very comforting.

Three hours later, Brock and the others are nearing the cave that he has seen before. It is a small cave and it hasn't been used for several years. One other problem is that no one knows how many men are at the cave. Are there just the four or could there be many more? Perhaps some were waiting at the cave or on a hunting trip and have now joined the kidnappers.

Brock and his men have no choice no matter what the odds. They must get the women back as quickly as possible. If they are right, as soon as the men that kidnapped the women are rested, they will have a joining ceremony. Then the women will be violated by whichever two men needs a wife. The clan could also be so barbaric that they might forgo a ceremony and just take the women. Ulda is only thirteen and has never been with a man. Tomah is a married woman and it would be a crushing blow to Durock and her both, if a man violated her.

Inside the cave, the four men have just arrived with the women and are sitting down resting. There are four other men with their wives and they seem pleased that the four have found two attractive women to add to the clan. There also are three small children and two older people, a man and a woman. Then there are two other women, which are the wives of two of the men that kidnapped Tomah and Ulda. These two women are kneeling near a fire holding some meat on a stick over the flames roasting it.

One of the kidnappers points to the meat and grunts. One of the women cooking the meat, which is his wife, stands up and brings it over to him. The second woman then gets up and brings the meat she's been roasting over to a second kidnapper, which is her husband. Now it becomes clear which men need a wife. The two single men keep looking over at Tomah and Ulda, grinning and whispering to one another. Tomah has a good idea what they are talking about but she wishes she didn't.

Just then, Tomah and Ulda hear a familiar voice. "Men in cave! Send Tomah and Ulda out!"

Suddenly, fear comes on every face inside the cave. The men jump to their feet and rush over and grab several spears that are leaning against the back wall. The women run to the rear of the cave and huddle together with the three small children. The eight men then go near the entrance of the cave.

One of the kidnappers peeks into the darkness and calls out, "No Tomah, no Ulda here! Go! Leave us."

Durock is furious and steps up beside Brock. "Send out my wife, Tomah, or all clan die!" he shouts.

Tomah can see that the men inside the cave are very afraid. They have no idea how many men are with Brock. Tomah then cries out, "Tomah here! Not many men inside cave. You have many strong men that kill great beasts! Come inside and kill little weak men!"

The men inside are now terrified. Their clan, like some Neanderthal clans, never hunt the mammoths. The men are too afraid to try to kill such a huge animal. They hunt smaller animals such as wild cattle and bison.

One of the kidnappers turns toward Tomah. "Tomah be one to die," he said, as he raises his spear. Before he can throw it, however, he hears a swishing sound and a spear comes from the darkness and hits him in the side. He has a shocked look on his face as he falls to the ground.

By the time he hits the ground, Brock and several of the men with him are at the cave entrance. The men inside are taken by surprise and both sides are throwing spears at one another. It only is a matter of a few seconds but everything happens as if it is in slow motion. Two more of the kidnappers are hit by spears from Brock's clan, but one of Brock's men is also hit. It is Garr. He has been hit in the chest and has fallen to the cave floor.

The men of the strange clan then drop their spears and run to the back of the cave where they huddle with the women and children. They do not want to fight any more. Tomah and Ulda get up and run over to Durock. Tomah hugs him, but he has his eyes on the men at the rear of the cave. Durock is still fuming mad. "Which men take Tomah," he asked, still looking back at the cowards.

Tomah points to the three men lying dead on the ground. "Those men take Ulda and me." She then turns and points to one of the men huddled with the others at the rear of the cave. "Other man there with women."

"Take me to man," he said, looking into her eyes.

Tomah begins walking to the back of the cave with Durock right behind her. When the last kidnapper sees them coming, he is terrified. When they get closer, he steps from behind the women and children and falls on his face, begging for his life.

Tomah stops just a few feet away, looks down at the man that's in the dirt sobbing and points. "*This* man that take Ulda and Tomah. Hit Ock with stick. Hit Gogg and women with stick."

Durock has no mercy and no compassion on a man that is so callous and so cold-hearted. Raising his spear, Durock draws his arm back behind his head. The man on the ground turns his head to look up and sees what is about to happen. He raises his left arm and shakes his head 'no', but it doesn't matter. Durock plunges the spear into the man's left side and the man falls back into the dust on the cave floor. The others that are huddled together near him scream out in horror at the sight. They believe they are to be next.

Durock, then takes hold of his spear and jerks it from the man's body, turns and walks over with Tomah to join Brock and the others. Brock and a couple of the men are taking the body of Garr outside when Durock and Tomah walks up to them at the entrance of the cave.

It is a happy time for Durock, Tomah and Ulda, but Soma, Garr's wife, will be devastated at the news of her husband's death.

Chapter 12

The Move

When Brock and the men return with Tomah and Ulda, along with Garr's body, there is gladness and sadness all at the same time. There are tears of joy for the women's return and many tears of sadness at the death of Garr. Soma, at just thirty-four, is now a widow.

After the men bury Garr's body Brock gives up a prayer to the Great Spirit. *"Great Spirit. Take Garr's spirit. Lead him to rivers of cool water, to valleys where there is warm sunshine. Let him be happy and full of life with you."*

With the prayer finished, the others look up into the sky and smile, all except Soma. She begins crying uncontrollably and Rena comes over and holds her.

The following day, Brock decides he should move the clan farther north. It would be better for Soma to have different scenery and they would be far away from the clan that took the women.

Crug does not want to go, however, and he makes his point clear. They are all sitting in the cave that morning when Brock tells every one of his plans to move. Upon hearing it, Crug becomes angry and stands to his feet. "Why Brock move clan?" he said, in an angry tone.

Brock looks over at him and can see the anger on his face. "Brock tell why. Be good for Soma. Be good for our people to be far away from others. Be good for hunting.

Many people in Brock's clan now. Need bigger cave for all people."

This does not sit well with Crug because it was his father, Ott, which brought the clan to this cave. "Father bring us here," he said, gesturing with his hands at the inside of the cave. "Cave been home for many seasons. People should not move."

Brock looks around at the others. He can see that some are not thrilled with the idea of moving either. "Father Ott make Brock leader," Brock said, tapping his chest with his finger tips and looking at each and every one there. Brock lead people to new cave. Make new home. People be happy there."

Everyone knows his word is law and they must obey whether they want to or not. Crug wants to go against him but he has second thoughts. Soma is in terrible grief and that is one of the reasons Brock wants to move. Crug is afraid if he tries to split the clan, most will not follow him.

It is the beginning of the summer season and they have all summer to find a new home. The next morning the weather is good and they have packed all their belongings on several travois and are ready to leave. On some of the travois, they have loaded long poles and several bison skins for teepee-like lodges. On some of the other travois, they have food, clothing and the men's hunting spears.

As they are leaving, everyone looks back at the cave. There is sadness because there have been so many good memories here. There is some joy, however, for what awaits them. They will be starting a new life in a new place. There is little joy for Soma, as she looks over at her husband's grave. As she is walking away, she stops and turns around. Tears are streaming down her face and she cannot help but run to the grave and fall down upon it. The other women see her and know Soma's heart is breaking and they run over to console her. The men stop and see what is going on and wait. Soma has taken the death of Garr harder than they thought she would. Her husband was her entire life and he was what she lived for. Now her world is gone and she faces a lonely existence without him. After several minutes, the other women finally get Soma to her feet and lead her way from the grave. Soma looks a mess with dirt all over her clothing and on her wet face from the many tears. Rena uses the bottom end of her deerskin skirt to wipe the dirt from her face and the tears from her eyes.

Once they are out of sight of the cave, Soma stops looking back and looks ahead. Rena continues walking beside her with her arm around her waist. Roosa is on the other side, also walking beside her. The women understand how it must feel to lose a husband. That is what a Neanderthal woman lives for — her husband and her children.

All summer, Brock and his people go north. Every few weeks they make a kill. When they do, they set up camp. While they are stopped, they roast the meat and dry some of it for jerky. Near the end of summer, Dearth and Graun are scouting a new area for game when they find a cave. It was hidden behind some bushes at the base of a small mountain. They were lucky to have spotted it because of the many rocks in front of the entrance.

As Dearth and Graun near the cave, they see that it appears to be a large one. Only the entrance is small because of the fallen rocks and they must climb over them to enter it. Once inside, it is very roomy and dry. At the back of the cave is a rock shelf, which would be perfect for storing things or even for sleeping. Above this shelf is a foot-wide vein of flint that runs all the way across the back of the cave. Cave dwellers of the past have chipped out pieces of the stone for their spear tips, skinning tools and to use to start fires. There is even a small spring seeping water in the corner that they can collect for drinking.

"Good cave," Dearth said, turning to Graun and grinning. "Brock will like cave."

Graun agrees and they hurry to tell Brock and the others what they have found.

Soon the entire clan is back at the cave. After Brock crawls over the rocks and steps inside, he is indeed pleased. "Good cave. Dearth good man," Graun said. "Plenty room for people."

The men then go about the task of moving the rocks in front of the cave so they can just walk in instead of climbing over them. When they are done, the women go to work inside the cave to make it feel like home. There is even a large crack in the ceiling so a fire will draw and before dark they have a fire built in the center of the cave floor.

This will be the clan's home for many years and many memories will be made here, some good, some bad. This is true not only for Neanderthals but for everyone. We must remember the good things and forget the bad. Otherwise, we could never enjoy life at all. That was the way the Neanderthal people looked at life those many years ago.

Chapter 13

The Savage Attack

After the clan settles in, life is good for a while. There is plenty of game nearby and everyone is pleased with their new home. Even Crug seems pleased, which is rare for him. Once they are finished moving in, Brock offers up a prayer to the Great Spirit. He thanks Him for finding a new home and for all the game that will feed the clan for many seasons to come.

As winter is nearing, the men are looking forward to hunting some mammoths. Several small herds have been seen just north of the cave. As life usually goes, however, the good times rarely last and then something dreadful happens. This was the case for this clan not long after they moved in.

Winter is almost upon them and many animals are starting to migrate south to find food. Others are just looking to find a warm place to spend the long cold months. This fact will soon change the lives of the entire clan.

It is only a few weeks after Brock has moved his people into the new cave. Everyone has been asleep for several hours and the sun is just coming up. The warm yellow rays are shining into the cave with most of the rays falling on Dearth's face. He awakens and when he opens his eyes, he is nearly blinded by the sunshine.

Squinting his eyes, he puts his hand on his forehead to keep the sun out and is about ready to throw off his bison hide when suddenly the sun's rays stop shining in his eyes. At first, he thinks someone has already gotten up and is standing between him and the cave entrance. A second later, however, fear grips his heart like a giant hand squeezing it. For right then, he hears the unmistakable huffing and blowing of a bear!

Everyone else in the cave is sound asleep. The fire has died down and they are all snuggled up under the covers. Then, unknown the Dearth, Brock must have been awakened by the sound of the bear, too. Throwing off his bison hide, Brock jumps to his feet as does Dearth. The commotion awakens everyone and soon the entire clan is up and on their feet.

There is confusion as to what is going on, especially by the women. The men know it is a bear that is standing just outside the entrance. This cave must have been where it hibernated the winter before and it has come back to it again.

Just then, the huge cave bear steps inside and begins looking around at all the people that is in *his* cave. There is no escape for the bear is blocking the entrance and he seems angry that others have dared take his winter home.

Brock turns his head and looks over at the men. "Put wood on fire!" he yelled.

Durock and Bogg toss several branches on the hot coals and the fire starts burning brighter. Dearth grabs a long stick and puts one end of it in the fire to light as a torch. By this time, the huge beast has walked into the cave a little further, which lets in some more light from the entrance. It is then that everyone can see how big the bear is and it is one of the largest they have ever seen.

Just then, the bear pins back his ears in anger and opens its enormous mouth, letting out a low, reverberating growl that echoes all throughout the cave.

"Kill it!" Brock yelled, as he grabs his spear that is leaning against the cave wall beside him.

All the men pick up their spears and at the same time launch them at the huge brown beast. Every one of the spears hits the giant bear, some in his side and others in his back. Instead of killing him or making him run from the cave, he roars out in pain and starts biting and snapping at the spears that have pierced his body. A moment later, he looks around at those in the cave, then rears up onto his hind legs, opens his mouth showing his huge sharp teeth and lets out another terrifying growl. Everyone is frozen in place at the awesome sight. Then, before the men can grab another spear, the bear drops back down on all fours and comes running toward Brock and Rena.

By this time, Brock has another spear in his hands, but the bear rushes right past him, knocking him to the ground and attacks his wife, Rena. With one massive bite, the bear's jaws clamp down on Rena's head. All those in the cave can hear the bones in her skull being crushed as the bear's teeth puncture her scalp. The huge bear then picks her up and shakes her like a rag doll before dropping her to the cave floor.

All this happens in an instant, even before Brock can get back on his feet. When he does get to his feet, he rushes up to the bear, takes his spear and with all his strength sticks it in into the bear's side, hoping to hit its lungs or heart. This, however, only enrages the bear more as it turns around and attacks him. With one powerful swipe, the bear's twelve-inch paw with six-inch claws knocks Brock to the ground and he tumbles several feet before hitting hard against the cave wall. The other men quickly throw their second spears at the bear. Most hit him, but since his back is to them, none penetrates his body enough to hit a vital organ.

When the bear is struck with more spears, he spins around to face the men. It is right then that Brock's two children, who were hiding under their covers, jump to their feet. The children are right between the bear and the other men. The movement of the children gets the bear's attention and he decides to take out his vengeance on them. With a short run, he jumps on the little boy, Trom, and bites down on his back. The bear's long canine teeth sink deep into the child's back and ribcage, puncturing his lungs and killing him almost instantly.

The little girl, Tuma, is so terrified that she just stands there screaming. The bear then leaves Trom's lifeless body and turns toward her. She doesn't stand a chance as the bear sweeps her up into his arms and bites down on her skull, crushing it like an eggshell.

By this time, Dearth has the torch lit and he rushes over toward the bear. The bear looks around, sees him coming, spins around and charges. It is almost upon him when it suddenly stops. The fire frightens him and he lets out a terrifying growl. The enraged bear seems disappointed that its bloody killing spree might be over. Then, something out the corner of the bear's left eye catches his attention. Brock is moving and trying to get back to his feet. This movement causes the bear to spin back around and focus his attention on Brock once again. Before the men can find any more spears, the bear rushes over and is on top of Brock, biting and ripping his flesh from the bones.

Dearth runs over with the torch to try and save him but it is too late. The bear, seeing the fire, backs away and looks around at all the men that are coming toward him screaming and throwing rocks. Then, looking toward the entrance, the bear runs from the cave with several spears still lodged in his back and sides.

Dearth, dropping the torch to the cave floor, kneels down beside Brock. He is still alive but barely. Dearth knows there is nothing he can do. The bear has caused too much damage and Brock has only minutes to live.

The other men have gathered around their leader and are standing there looking down at his torn, mangled and bloody body. The women are all crying and looking at the bodies of Rena and her children.

As Brock is drawing his last breathes, he looks around at the men standing above him. He then looks up at Dearth. When their eyes meet, Brock reaches for the necklace that is hanging around his neck and pulls it off. Holding it up to Dearth he says, "You are now leader of our people."

Dearth does not know what to say.

Brock then struggles to get more words out. "Dearth be good leader," he said, with a slight smile. He then closes his eyes and lets out his last breath.

Dearth looks around at the others who are just as surprised as he is. He can see that Crug is angry, but Brock and Brock alone had the power to determine who the next leader would be. Evidently, he saw something in Dearth that made him choose him. Crug will just have to get over it.

Later, the men track the bear and find it dead, but his death comes much too late to save an entire family. To this day, the bear's skull is kept in the cave with the clan to remember that awful attack.

Chapter 14

The Good News

Dearth now has a lot of responsibility on his broad shoulders. He is clan leader and every one of his people depends on his decisions to have peace and prosperity in their lives. He seems to take the responsibility in stride, however, and goes on as if he has always been the leader. That is the reason Brock believed he would be the best choice to lead the clan.

Only a few weeks after becoming the new leader, he receives some good news. His wife, Serna, is pregnant and is looking forward to having their first child.

Dearth has been going through a difficult time with the death of Brock and his family, but this news cheers him up. He has been looking forward to the day he could have a son and teach him all he knows. Dearth understands that the child could be a girl and he would love her but he is hoping for a boy.

Serna knows that Dearth would like to have a son first but she only hopes the baby is healthy. She would be pleased, however, if she could give her husband the desire of his heart and present him with a son. Only time will tell, but for today both are overjoyed that they will become parents in the not-too-distant future.

Chapter 15

The Breaking of Dawn

It is now a few months later and it's time for Kuma to have her first child. It's the month of the third moon, which would be late May or early June on today's calendar. Kuma goes into labor late one night right after she and Graun go to bed. All the women of the clan stay up during the night with her, but the men sleep the entire night through, or at least they try to. It is not always easy to sleep with a woman crying out in labor pains. Graun of course does not even try to go to sleep. He stays close by waiting for the baby to come into the world.

Roosa is again the acting midwife and is there beside Kuma encouraging her. Kuma's labor lasts all night but as the dawn is breaking, Kuma delivers a tiny baby girl. Graun is somewhat disappointed that it wasn't a boy, but happy that the baby seems to be healthy and that Kuma made it through the delivery without any complications.

Kuma already has a name picked out, as is the custom if the baby is a girl. After the baby is born, however, she changes her mind and names the baby Ee'na, which means the breaking of dawn. The baby has lots of hair, a wide nose and rather short arms and legs, a typical Neanderthal infant. She seems to be very heathy and is soon at her mother's breasts eating her first meal.

Graun is very proud to be a father and all that day he is smiling and talking about his daughter. Kuma is also very happy and every girl and woman in the clan wants to hold the tiny baby.

Durr and Ulda are next in line to be joined and Ulda can hardly wait until she, too, is married and has a baby of her own.

Chapter 16

Durr and Ulda Joined

Now that Dearth is the leader, he will be the one performing any joining ceremonies. It has been only a couple of months since Kuma had her baby and Dearth is more than happy to see his clan growing. Today, he will join the latest couple, which will be seventeen-year-old Durr and fifteen-year-old Ulda.

All that day the couple is full of joy. The women are helping Ulda get ready for her joining ceremony and the men are teasing Durr about his wedding night. Just like all the ones joined before, the bride will be dressed in her finest clothing, with a newly made necklace and red ocher on her face.

The groom will also be dressed in his best with his spear at his side. One of the women, which is always the oldest and is Roosa, will present two pieces of roasted meat to Dearth. He will give one piece each to the couple. They will place the small piece of meat in the other's mouth to signify that they will take care of one another. The spear that the groom holds signifies that he will provide food for his wife and children. After the ceremony there is dancing and rejoicing, long into the night.

When the time comes for the joining ceremony, everyone gathers around a big fire that is several feet outside the cave entrance. If it was winter, they would have the ceremony inside, but since it is warm weather, it will take place outdoors.

The bride and groom are all smiles as the ceremony begins. Durr has sweaty palms as he takes Ulda's hand. This is the first joining ceremony Dearth has performed and he is a little nervous. He has seen enough of them to know what to do, however. Everything goes off without a hitch and after Dearth gives the bride and groom a hug, they are officially joined and will be until one of them dies.

It has been a good day and everyone is full of joy and many rejoice nearly till dawn with dancing, storytelling and eating. While the others are outside, Durr and Ulda sneak off to the cave to consummate their marriage.

Chapter 17

The Great Disappointment

After the joining of Durr and Ulda, things are going well for Dearth. He and his wife, Serna, have a child on the way and Serna's time is fast approaching. By now, Serna's belly is very large and she has difficulty sitting and getting back up. She is overjoyed, however, that her time is nearly here.

The sun has just come up late that autumn when Dearth and the men are getting ready to go on a hunt for bison. The bison are migrating south before winter sets in and a large herd has been spotted just west of the cave.

The men grab some left over roasted wild boar meat to take with them and are about to leave when Serna has her first contraction. She had just gotten out of bed and was going over to say good-bye to her husband when it hit.

Dearth sees her coming over to him and then sees her put her hands on her belly and is grimacing from the pain.

Quickly Dearth lays his spears down against a large rock and hurries over to her. "Baby come?" he asked.

Serna looks up into his face and smiles. "Baby come."

Dearth looks over at Roosa, who is hugging her husband, Nagar. "Roosa," Dearth calls. "Serna's baby come!"

Roosa turns around and sees the concern on Dearth's face and smiles. "I go help Serna," she tells Nagar. "You be careful on hunt."

"No worry. You help with baby," he answers back.

Roosa nods and goes over to help Serna sit down. "Come, sit," Roosa said, taking Serna by the arm and leading her to the rear of the cave.

Dearth follows them and has a seat on a large rock beside his wife.

Once Serna is comfortable, Roosa turns to Dearth. "Could be long wait for baby to come. Dearth could go on hunt. Be back before baby born."

Dearth shakes his head. "Dearth stay. See baby when born."

Roosa smiles, knowing Dearth would not leave. He has been waiting for this baby to be born for a long time and he doesn't want to leave Serna's side until it is here.

All day Serna is in labor and things seem to be going all right. Later that afternoon, however, Roosa begins to get worried. She does not want Serna to know she is worried but Serna can sense it herself. Dearth, too, is very concerned and is still nearby waiting for the baby to come into the world.

Looking up as she is squatting down between the two large rocks, Serna asked, "Why baby not come?"

Roosa shakes her head. "Baby come soon. No worry."

An hour later, however, both women know something is terribly wrong. Dearth is beside himself with worry and he goes outside to walk around. It is difficult for him to watch his wife suffer.

Once he has left the cave, Roosa has Serna to lie down. She will have to reach in and determine if the baby is in the correct position. The other women are standing nearby and O'ma, Augg's wife, is kneeling down beside her holding Serna's hand. When Roosa reaches in and touches the baby, she knows instantly what is wrong. The baby is in a breach position when it should have its head in the birth canal.

Roosa looks up at Serna's face, which is covered in sweat. "Baby not have head in right place. I try to move baby to face right way."

Serna nods as Roosa reaches back up and tries to turn the baby around. It takes several long minutes but finally the baby is turned. "Baby right way now," Roosa said. "Baby come soon."

Ten minutes later, Roosa sees its head. She smiles and looks again at Serna. "Baby's head come. Be born soon."

Serna manages a slight smile then bares her teeth when another sharp labor pain hits. She can feel the baby move further down and she knows it is almost there.

As the baby comes from the womb, Roosa catches it in her hands and immediately takes it over to a pile of skins and lays it down. She can see that it is not breathing and is blue. Grabbing a soft deerskin, she begins rubbing it all over trying to get it to take a breath. She already knows, however, that it has been without air too long.

Serna, lifting herself up onto her elbows, looks to see what is going on. She can see that the baby is not moving. "What wrong?" she asked.

Roosa stops trying to revive the baby, turns around and looks at Serna. Roosa hates to tell her but she knows she must. "Baby not breathing. Baby dead."

Serna falls back down onto her back and begins to cry bitterly. The women come to her side trying to comfort her, she can't be consoled.

Right then Dearth walks in, sees her crying and rushes over to her side. He knows something is wrong even before he reaches her, because he sees the baby lying nearby partially covered with the deerskin and it is not moving.

When Dearth kneels down and takes her hand, Serna looks up through the veil of tears. "Baby born dead!"

Dearth nods and gives her a smile. "Serna have more babies."

Serna nods but Dearth can see his words do not comfort her any. He later learns the baby was a little boy and he had already picked out a name, but he would have to wait until next time to use it. The name he had chosen was Braum but it will be a long time before he will have another son.

Dearth buries the baby and is very disappointed that it was stillborn. His disappointment, however, was nothing compared to Serna's. She is very depressed and seems not to care about anything anymore. She won't eat right and just a few days afterwards she falls ill. No one knows what it is but her fever becomes so high that she becomes delirious and is talking out of her head. Three days later she dies.

Dearth is crushed. He not only lost a son that he had wanted for a long time, but he has now lost the love of his life, as well. He doesn't speak of it but everyone knows he is devastated.

Neanderthal men rarely cry and when they do, they never want anyone to see them. Dearth will often take long walks and be gone for several hours. Everyone knows he is grieving but no one says a word. He will have to come to grips with the great loss himself.

Dearth is only twenty-three years old and a widower. He was married for just six years and is now alone without a mate. The clan still depends on him and he must continue being the leader no matter how much sorrow he feels. He knows the sorrow will subside someday and he will be happy again, but right now that seems like an eternity away.

Chapter 18

A New Love?

The months go by and it is learned that Durr and Ulda are going to have a child, which is good news to the growing clan. Dearth's sorrow over the loss of his wife, Serna, has also subsided and he begins feeling almost normal again. After losing Serna, he never thought the weight from his heart would ever be lifted. But as the weeks turned into months, it felt as though there would be small rays of sunshine that would lighten his heart from time to time. He knew then the grief was lessening and finally it was nearly gone.

One day, as he is coming in from a hunt, fifteen-year-old Ursa meets him at the cave entrance with a smile. She has come over to him to take the meat he is carrying and will help the other women cut it up into steaks and thin strips for jerky.

Unknown to Dearth, Ursa has had a crush on him for the last two years. She knew there was no hope of ever having him as a husband, but when Serna died her hopes came alive. She has not wanted to let him know how she felt until his time of grieving was over, but today she thought she would let him know that she is interested.

Ursa has developed into a pretty woman during the past year. Her breasts are full, her long, curly dark brown hair reaches all the way down to her waist and she has an infectious smile.

When she smiles at Dearth, he looks deep into her dark brown eyes and sees them sparkle. He smiles back and Ursa lowers her head, and then lifts her eyes looking up at him to let him know she likes him. From this moment on, they are together quite often and in only a month he wants to take her as his wife.

Since Dearth is the leader and does all the joining ceremonies, he must choose another man to do the honors. His first choice is Crug as he is the oldest son of the former leader, Ott. Crug, however, declines, which Dearth halfway expected. Crug still has much resentment and animosity because his father did not make him leader. He has even more anger now because Brock made Dearth the new leader instead of him.

The honor of performing the joining ceremony then falls on Augg as he is the oldest man in the clan. Augg is more than happy to do it and before the day is over Dearth and Ursa are joined in marriage. This is the happiest Dearth has been since before Serna passed away. Everyone can see the change since Ursa has come into his life and they are happy for him. Perhaps now things can get back to normal.

Chapter 19

Ulda's Disappointment

A few weeks after Dearth and Ursa are joined, another couple faces a fiery trial. Ulda and Durr have been looking forward to having their first child, but when Ulda is awakened with labor pains in the middle of the night, she knows something is not right.

Turning over toward Durr she nudges him awake. "What want?" he said, still half asleep.

"Baby come," she replied.

This gets Durr's attention and he jumps up from under the bison skin and looks at her. "Not time for baby to come," he said. He can see the worry in her eyes even in the dem light of the fire that has died down. "I wake Roosa. Roosa know what to do."

Ulda nods and Durr goes over to where Roosa and Nagar are sleeping. "Roosa," Durr said, as he leans over her sleeping form.

Roosa knows something is wrong when she hears him call her. Rolling over, she looks up at the worry on his face. "What need?"

"Ulda's baby come."

"Not time for baby," she said, crawling out from under the covers.

Her husband, Nagar, awakens. "What wrong?" he asked.

"Ulda having baby. Go back to sleep."

Nagar, still half asleep, rolls over and is soon sound asleep again.

Roosa comes over with Durr to Ulda's side and kneels down beside her. "Pains bad?" Roosa asked.

"Some pains bad. Some not bad," Ulda answers.

Roosa places her right hand on Ulda's belly and keeps it there until she has another contraction. When it hits, Ulda moans in pain.

Roosa looks over at Durr. "Baby come soon."

Ulda is very concerned, however. "Not time for baby. What wrong?"

"Not know," Roosa replied. "Sometime baby come early. We not know why till baby born."

Ulda nods, knowing there is nothing to do but have the baby and hope everything is all right. It is two months early and it is rare for a premature Neanderthal baby to survive born at seven months.

The first rays of dawn are beginning to break when Ulda's labor pains become very close together. Everyone is waking up to the sound of her moaning. The others are surprised that she is having the baby so soon, and they know that something must be wrong. Durr is sitting nearby watching and is hoping for the best.

An hour later, Roosa tells Ulda that she can see the baby's head and, in another moment, Roosa is holding the tiny three-pound baby in her hands. It is a little girl but she is not breathing and it looks as if she has been dead for at least a couple of days.

"Is baby good?" Ulda asked, as Roosa turns around so Ulda cannot see it lifeless body.

Roosa does not answer right away but places the baby down on a deerskin and covers it. She then turns to Ulda. "Baby not live. Baby born dead."

Durr is already standing and comes over and kneels at Ulda's side. He does not know what to say but lays his big calloused hand on her arm to comfort her.

Ulda looks up at him with tears in her eyes. "Baby not live. Come too early."

Durr nods and pats her arm. "Ulda have more babies. Many babies that live."

It takes Ulda several weeks to feel even partially healthy again. She was so hoping to have a child for Durr. It was a girl and she wanted to name her Mulda but it was not meant to be. It almost seemed that the clan had a curse on it. Two babies in a row that were stillborn.

Chapter 20

Double Trouble

Several months later, it is learned that Ulda is pregnant again and this time she is hoping things will be different. It is also learned that Dearth and Ursa are expecting their first child. Both women are elated. Their babies will be born within a few weeks of one another and the women spend much time talking about their babies growing up together.

The months pass slowly for the two women. Both are anxious for their babies to be born. When their due dates are near, Ulda is very excited. Her last baby came early and was stillborn. This time, her pregnancy is full term and everything seems to be going great.

Ursa also has had no complications and as spring is arriving, Ursa goes into labor first. It is early morning when the labor pains start and Dearth is right there beside her. His first wife Serna was never able to give him a child, he is looking forward to being a father, and he is secretly hoping it will be a boy.

The men of the clan have placed two large boulders close together at the rear of the cave. This is so when a woman is delivering a child, she can squat down between them, placing her arms around on both sides for support. This squatting position is the natural way to have a baby so that gravity can help the baby move through the birth canal.

The boulder also gives the woman something to grab hold of when the contractions become intense.

Dearth is sitting close by at the beginning of the delivery but after several minutes decides he needs some air and goes outside with the other men. The women are there to care for Ursa and he leaves it to them to help his wife with her delivery.

Ursa's labor is relatively easy and two hours after her water breaks, she has the baby. Dearth is still outside the cave talking with Ock and the other men when he hears the baby cry. Upon hearing the cries, he stops speaking in mid-sentence and turns toward the cave entrance. "Baby come," he said, his eyes lighting up. "Must see if baby is boy," and he hurries into the cave.

Ursa in lying on a pallet made of several bison hides holding the baby on her breasts when Dearth approaches. He can't see the sex of the baby because it is face down.

When Ursa sees him walk up she looks up and smiles. "Dearth father," she said.

Dearth smiles back and nods.

Ursa knows Dearth is very anxious to know if it is a boy or a girl and she deliberately makes him wonder a minute longer. Finally, she looks into his eyes and gives him another slight grin. "Dearth want boy or girl?" she teasingly asked.

Dearth does not know how to answer because the question catches him off guard. "Dearth want boy," he said. "Woman want girl. Dearth be happy for wife, if girl. Be happy for Dearth, if boy."

Ursa then has a big grin as she lifts the baby and turns it so Dearth can see that it is a boy. "Wife give husband boy," she said, looking into her husband's widened eyes.

"Boy be great hunter someday," he proudly said.

"What name for boy?" Ursa asked.

Dearth grins, looks down at the newborn then at Ursa. "Name is Braum. Braum good name," he said. "Be good name for great man."

Ursa nods in agreement and lays the baby back on her breasts so he can go back to sleep. Both baby and Ursa are very tired and Dearth leaves them to rest and goes outside to tell the men that he is now the father of a son.

Ulda has been there the entire time watching Ursa deliver the baby and seeing Dearth's and Ursa's joy. She is very happy for them and can hardly wait until she has her baby, so she and Durr can also have that much happiness.

Chapter 21

The Heartbreak

Two weeks later, Ulda goes into labor. Her labor is a little more difficult than Ursa's was, but normal. After eight hours of labor, she delivers a little boy and she and Durr are elated. They name him Drock and both parents are very happy, as is the entire clan. Ulda had lost her first child for it was premature and stillborn. Now, she has brought one to full term and it is a boy just as Durr wanted. There will now be two new hunters in the clan in a few years and the boys will grow up together. She knows that Braum and Drock will someday be great men. Durr, too, is very proud to have a son and he and Dearth brag about how great their sons will be someday.

Right after little Drock is born, however, Roosa sees that something is wrong. He does not seem to be breathing right and he doesn't want to nurse very much. Ulda is beside herself with worry but there is nothing she can do. The baby continues to go downhill and seven days later, he dies.

The entire clan is shocked but not as much as Ulda. The women try to comfort her but she cannot be consoled and she goes into a deep depression. It takes months for her to come out of it and she never seems to be the same again.

By this time, many in the clan are certain there is a curse on them. Three out of four babies have died. They are beginning to be afraid of what the future may hold.

This is only the beginning of the troubles that lie ahead. If they knew all that was going to happen, they would be even more afraid.

Chapter 22

Braum

Little Braum grows like a weed and in just nine months he is trying to speak. He can say a few words and he understand even more. He understands the words, eat, go outside, and of course, the words for mother and father. The first word he learned, however, was "NO!" This was because as soon as he was able, he started to get into things. No one had ever seen a baby learn so much so quickly. At ten months of age, he is pulling up to things and trying to take his first steps. By twelve months, he is toddling around the cave getting into things and it is a full-time job for his mother, Ursa, to watch him.

His father, Dearth, is already spoiling his little boy. He plays with him every morning and evenings after returning from each hunt. He has already made him a tiny spear for him to practice with; that is as soon as he is big enough to throw it. Ursa loves seeing Dearth interacting with their son and she couldn't be any happier.

Ulda, however, is still going through a deep depression and even though she is happy for Ursa and Dearth having little Braum, she still grieves over the loss of her baby, Drock. Durr assures her that she will have another child and it will live, but each month that she does not become pregnant, she sits and cries and is depressed even more. There is nothing anyone can do but let time heal her broken heart. Everyone in the clan is hoping she becomes pregnant soon and has a baby that she wants so badly.

Other than the problem with Ulda, everything else with the clan is great. There is much game and the men have been successful on every hunt and without any of them being injured. Winter has just set in and only last week the men killed a large mammoth, the meat of which will last them all winter.

As soon as Ursa roasts the first mammoth steaks, Dearth wants to give some to Braum. Taking the baby in his arms, he walks over to a large rock by the fire and sits down. After placing Braum on his lap, he sees that Ursa has some done. "Give small piece to Braum."

Ursa turns to Dearth with a questioning look. "Baby have no teeth. How baby eat meat?"

"Dearth have teeth. I chew meat for baby Braum."

"Give just little," Ursa advises handing Dearth a tiny sliver no larger than the tip of his little finger.

Taking the hot piece of mammoth meat from her hand, Dearth blows on it to cool it before putting it in his mouth. After he thoroughly chews it, he takes the tiny piece from his mouth and puts it to Braum's lips. "Eat," he said, smiling. "Meat make Braum strong like father."

Braum looks up at his father's face and grins as he opens his little mouth. Dearth takes his fingers and puts the chewed-up meat inside. As he begins chewing it, little Braum makes a face as he tastes solid food for the first time.

"Meat good," Dearth said, grinning and then looking over at Ursa.

Ursa smiles. "One more piece and no more," she said. "No want baby sick."

"One more," Dearth replied, taking the tiny hunk of meat and blowing on it before chewing it for the baby.

As Ursa and Dearth sit there that night, they have high hopes that Braum will have a long and prosperous life. This is the wish of all parents. They do not know what the future holds just as parents today. If they could look ahead, they would see that it will be nothing like they could ever have imagined.

Chapter 23

Ulda's Good News

Near the end of that winter, Ulda has some good news. She is pregnant again! She has been depressed for months and some in the clan thought she may never come out of it.

When she realizes she is going to have another baby, she is elated but fearful at the same time. After having two babies that have not survived, Ulda is understandably concerned that she will also lose this one. Durr tries to assure her that it will be a healthy baby but Ulda is very apprehensive. As the pregnancy progresses, however, much of her fears subsides and she is feeling better than she has since she lost Drock.

Not much else is happening. Everyone is looking forward to the summer months. The youngsters, especially can't wait until it is warm enough to take off their shoes and run barefoot outside. They do inside, but it is not the same. They love to feel the cool grass between their toes and wade in shallow pools of water. The children can just be children without a care in the world. They run and play all day. There will be plenty of time for taking on responsibility when they get a little older. Right now, they just love being a child.

The adults, too, are anxious for summer to arrive. Dearth will take the clan north following the migrating herds to their calving grounds. The summers are short but full of excitement and adventure. If the clan members knew what would happen even before they get to head north, they would be shocked. That, however, is the way life goes, especially for Neanderthals.

Chapter 24

O'ma

Once Ulda learns she is pregnant and spring is just around the corner, the entire clan is in a very cheerful mood. Winter has been long and cold and the women have been confined to the cave for much of that time. The men, too, often are stuck inside during the harshest part of the winter, only going out on hunts when they have to.

Then, just three weeks before the weather breaks for good, there is a warm spell and everyone goes outside into the fresh air.

The men go north to catch some fish in the river, which is now running from the melting snows. It has been a long time since they have had fresh fish. Mammoth meat gets old very quickly and fish will be a welcome change.

While the men are on their fishing trip, the women go outside to do a host of chores. Some are gathering firewood, while others are scraping two deer hides the men brought back a few days earlier.

Augg's wife, O'ma, takes two water bags and heads down to a small stream to fill them. It is not far and she has gone there many times before, so she has no concern of any danger. This day, however, will be different from any other.

Upon reaching the stream, O'ma lays one water bag down as she lowers the second one into the water. No sooner has she submerged the neck of the water bag in the water, she hears something behind her. Looking over her left shoulder, she is stunned to see two large dire wolves standing there watching her. The wolves look very lean and she knows they must be starving. Often, the winters kill many animals and the scavengers have plenty of food. During other winters, few animals die and it is hard for the predators and scavengers to find enough to eat. This is one of those winters.

Before O'ma can get to her feet, the two wolves rush toward her, knock her down and begin savagely biting her arms and legs. O'ma screams at the top of her lungs for help, but the wolves continue their merciless attack. Soon the ground is covered in blood and her flesh is hanging in long strips from her arms and legs as the two wolves are eating her alive!

O'ma's body goes into shock and everything seems unreal, as if she is in a bad dream. A moment later, she hears the voices of women screaming and sees the wolves out the corner of her eye moving away. The next thing she sees is Ursa leaning over her. That is the last thing she remembers until she awakens in the cave with Augg sitting beside her.

It is dark inside the cave with only the light of the fire, but even in the dim light, she can see tears in Augg's eyes as he looks down at her. Augg has seen what the wolves did before O'ma was covered in the warm bison hides. He knows his wife has no chance of living; there has been just too much damage done to her body. She has also lost a lot of blood and he is amazed that she has hung on this long.

O'ma moves her lips trying to speak but the words do not come. Augg leans over so that he can hear if she is able to whisper and he hears her mumble, "I sorry."

Augg shakes his head. "O'ma good woman. Not need to be sorry for anything."

O'ma manages a slight smile as she closes her eyes and goes unconscious once again. As Augg sits there looking at her, his life with O'ma runs through his mind. He remembers how she looked when they were young, right after they first married. He remembers her laughter, her joy when he returned from dangerous hunts. He remembers the long winters and warm summers she walked beside him. Now she is slipping further away by the minute.

Augg looks at her face as she is lying there. O'ma is just thirty-eight years old but she looks much older than her years. She never was a robust woman as Neanderthals go. For some unknown reason, she could never bear children or even become pregnant. Augg always wanted children but he never let O'ma know how much. He loved her and let on like it was not a great disappointment that she couldn't give him a child. She knew, however, how much he wanted a son.

Augg's heart feels very heavy as he reaches and takes her small hand in his. He remembers all the times her hands cooked him meals and rubbed his aching shoulders after carrying large pieces of meat for miles after a hunt. He remembers the times her arms held him when he made love to her and the joy on her face when they became one.

While these things are going through his mind, O'ma opens her eyes once again, looks up and says, "Augg, my husband." She then smiles and closes her eyes for the last time.

Augg just sits there looking at the peace that is on her face and knows she is gone forever. Now he must face life alone. Inside, his heart is breaking and a sadness like he has never known before comes over him. Getting up, he walks toward the cave entrance. The others see him get up, walk away, and know O'ma has died. They do not say a word but watch as Augg goes outside in the darkness.

From this day forward, the light of his life is gone and his days that remain will never be as bright as before. O'ma and Augg had been married since she was a young woman of just fourteen and he was seventeen. Now Augg will have to live the rest of his life without her there beside him. Augg is forty-one years old and the way his heart feels, he is wishing he could be laid in a grave beside the love of his life and not go on without her.

O'ma was a good woman and Augg knows he was lucky to have had her all the years he did. That is not very comforting, however, it only makes her loss that much more painful.

Chapter 25

The Rhino Incident

Augg has just turned forty-two-years-old for he was born in early spring. Another year in his lonely life is not important, however. It just means another year without his wife, O'ma, beside him.

It is just a month after O'ma's death and Augg is still very much grieving for his beloved wife, but life goes on and he has duties he must perform. The most important of which is going on hunts to provide meat for the clan.

The entire clan has gone north to hunt the herds that are going to their calving grounds. They are camped several miles north of the river. The hunt they are going on today is to be a hunt like many others before it. What happens this day, however, will change the lives of many, most especially, Augg.

The men do not know what they will hunt today. Hunting for the Neanderthals is a game of chance and opportunity. Whatever they find, that is what they will hunt. They are hoping to find a bison or reindeer herd but fate will deal them a different hand.

There are ten men in the hunting party as they head north of the river. This is where the bison and reindeer herds have been seen over the last several days. The men are hoping to kill at least two of whichever they come across today.

When they get near the place the herds were seen a day before, there is not a single animal in sight. "Herds go farther north," Dearth said, pointing with his spear.

The men stand for a moment searching the northern horizon for any movement, but see nothing. The men walk a short distance and begin to find thousands of bison tracks. After following them for a while, the tracks turn and start going southwest. Dearth thinks the herd must be heading back to the river to drink. "Bison go to river," Dearth said. "We follow."

An hour later, they are nearing the river. Upon reaching the riverbank, the men see that the herd has stopped to drink, then have headed upstream. After seeing this, Dearth leads the men along the shore hoping to catch up with them.

The hunting party hasn't gone a mile when Ock's sharp eyes see something about a hundred yards ahead. Looking over to Dearth, Ock points to what he sees. "There," he whispers. "Rhino on ground."

Dearth sees it and nods. It is a large woolly rhino lying in some bushes near the riverbank. The other men see it, too, and Dearth motions for the men to stay down and sneak closer.

Using the bushes as cover, the men cautiously sneak along the riverbank until they are about fifty yards away. Dearth turns to Augg, Crug, Bogg and Brant. "Go around and come up on other side," he whispers. "We wait till you there, then we come."

The men nod and make a wide swing so they can get on the other side of the sleeping rhino. This way it will be between them. Once the men are in place, Dearth and those with him will come closer, so they can spear the huge beast.

Everything goes according to plan. Crug, Augg, Bogg and Brant get around to the other side and are waiting for Dearth and his men to sneak closer. If the rhino spooks and heads away from Dearth, then Crug and the three men with him will be in position to spear it as it goes right past them.

Ever so carefully, Dearth and his men sneak up behind the rhino. When they are just a few yards away, they clutch their spears tightly in their right hands and prepare to throw them. Dearth is out front. When he is just a few steps away from the snoozing rhino, he raises his spear and with all his might throws it at the rhino's upper ribcage. The spear sails the short distance and sinks deep into the rhino's thick hide.

When the spear hits, the rhino bellows out in pain, jumps to his feet and spins around to his right then to his left, trying to locate what has attacked him. The men with Dearth are downwind, so the poor-sighted animal cannot smell them. It does get the scent of Crug and the three men however that are with him.

The men with Dearth launch their spears and all hit the rhino, but most hit him in the back and rear, which does little damage. Once he is hit again, he is filled with rage and starts charging toward the strange smell of the humans that are upriver.

Crug and Augg are in front of Bogg and Brant, but they all see what has happened and now the rhino is coming right toward them. All four men raise their spears and as the rhino is nearly upon them, they throw them. Two of the spears hit the shaggy beast in the left side of his neck; Brant's spear misses, and Augg's spear hits the rhino in the side, sinking deep between his ribs. This is a fatal blow, but it will take time for the huge animal to die.

When he is hit, he turns to his left and runs right at the men. When he is right on top of Crug and Bogg, the men leap to the side just in time to keep its four-foot horn from impaling them. Augg and Brant are also able to jump out of the way, but the rhino spins around and rushes toward Augg while he is still on the ground. Before he can get up and run out of the way, the rhino lowers its head and rams into him as he is struggling to his feet. The impact knocks him back down onto the ground, causing him to drop his other spear. Then with another rush, the rhino pins Augg to the ground crushing his right hip.

By this time, all the men are there and throw their second spears. When the spears strike the angry rhino, it breaks off its attack and runs away. It looks like a pincushion with all the spears sticking out of its body as the men watch its retreat. They know it won't get far before succumbing to its wounds, but right now Augg needs tending to.

Augg is conscious when the men come to his side, but he is in a lot of pain. His hip is out of the socket and his upper thighbone is broken. Dearth tells Ock and Durr to get two sticks for a splint for the broken bone as he prepares to shove the hipbone back into the socket.

Kneeling down beside Augg, Dearth raises up the bison robe that covers Augg's hip and right leg. Placing his hands on Augg's hip, he looks into his eyes. "Hip out of socket."

Augg nods, knowing what is coming, and grits his teeth. With a sudden jerk, Dearth pulls the hip bone back into place and it slips into the socket. Augg cannot help but cry out from the intense pain but the worst is over or so he hopes.

Once Ock and Durr are back with the splints, Dearth sets the leg, which is nearly as painful as putting the hip back into the socket. After wrapping several long pieces of rawhide around the splints, Dearth tells Augg to lie there and rest until the men can make a travois, so they can get him back to camp.

This is a day that will forever change Augg's life. The leg will heal but he will be crippled for the rest of his life and this is the last hunt he will ever go on.

Chapter 26

The Neighbors

Two days after Augg's incident with the woolly rhino, which left him crippled, Dearth and his hunting party are going back to retrieve what meat is left on the carcass. On the way there, they see another Neanderthal hunting party of six along the river. An older man leads it by the name of Drog.

Upon seeing Dearth and his men, Drog holds his spear above his head, as do the men with him. This is to signify that they are friendly. As Dearth approaches, Drog looks Dearth's men over, nods, then grins revealing he has many teeth missing.

When Dearth is a few feet away, Drog steps forward with a noticeable limp and sticks his spear in the ground. "Drog from south," he said, pointing at himself then toward the south as he looks at Dearth then over at the others with him. "We hunt bison."

Dearth looks at the old man and the first thing he notices is that he has long nasty scars on the left side of his face from his forehead to his chin and also on his left arm. It looks as if he had tangled with a cave bear at one point in time or perhaps a saber-tooth cat. He is wearing an old worn-out bison skin around his lower body and his long bushy beard has some gray in it as does his long, matted reddish brown hair. "I Dearth. We from south, too. Come to get meat from rhino we kill two sunsets ago."

Drog nods then squints into the sunshine as he looks into Dearth's eyes. "Rhino big?" he asked.

Dearth nods. "Much big."

"Much meat left?"

Dearth understands by the question that the old man must need the meat. "Some meat left," Dearth replied.

"Leader Dearth share meat?" Drog asked.

Dearth looks at the old man then over at the men that are with him and nods. "We share what is left."

The old man seems very pleased as do the men with him.

"Kill far?" Drog asked, as he and his men start following Dearth upstream.

"Not far. Just little way."

On the way there, Dearth learns that there is to be a spring rendezvous at the next full moon, which is three weeks away. Dearth and his clan have not been to a rendezvous since they moved north to the new cave. During a rendezvous, clans from the surrounding area come to trade hides, spear points, spears, tools and other things. Often, the men and women find a mate while they are there. Ock and Gogg both do not have a woman in the clan the right age to marry and when they hear of the rendezvous, they are thrilled.

After Drog gives directions to where the rendezvous will be held, Dearth tells Drog that they will be there. Drog is happy that they ran into Dearth, for they hadn't made a kill for three moons and their meat is nearly gone.

When arriving at the rhino carcass, most of the meat has already been cut from the bones but Drog is pleased to get anything. He and his men stand to the side and wait until

Dearth and his men take what they want from the dead rhino. Dearth does not take all that he had planned on taking, seeing that Drog and his clan must need the meat very badly. When he has cut several pieces from the carcass, he stops and looks at his men. "We have enough," he said, and he takes the hunk of meat he has in his hand and walks away.

Crug seems a little angry that Dearth is going to let Drog take what is left, when there is much more meat that can be salvaged from the rhino. "There's more meat," he said, looking over at Dearth.

"We have enough," Dearth said, with firmness. "We go now."

Crug looks at Dearth with disdain, then grabs the meat from the ground that he has cut and storms off with it.

Dearth watches him for a second, then steps away from the carcass and looks over at Drog. "You take rest of meat."

Drog smiles, then and he and his men hurry to cut what is left from the bones. They even take many of the bones so they can dig the marrow from inside. The next day they return to take the head and any other scraps the scavengers may have left behind.

When Dearth and his hunting party return to camp, he tells the others about the upcoming rendezvous and all are looking forward to it. Everyone that is, except for Augg. He cannot walk and his hip and leg are giving him fits of pain.

Dearth offers to take him along on a travois but Augg knows the jarring would not be pleasant and he couldn't enjoy the trip with all the pain he's suffering. He tells Dearth he will stay behind and wait until the clan returns. Dearth then says that he will have one the women stay with Augg to take care of his needs.

Since Augg's accident, Dearth decides leave the summer camp and return to the cave. It will be much better for Augg than living in temporary shelters and moving all the time. Dearth believes he and his men can find enough game until the herds return in the fall. Augg is thankful that Dearth cares about him as do the others, but his heart is still empty and nothing can fill the deep void he feels after losing his wife.

Chapter 27

The Rendezvous

As the day of the rendezvous nears, everyone in Dearth's clan is excited. Not since Brock was the leader, have they been to one, and that was far to the south. Everyone there will be strangers except for the six men that Dearth's hunting party met and he barely knows them.

By this time, Augg can actually hobble around a little and his pain has somewhat subsided, so he tells Dearth he has decided that he wants to come along. Dearth is happy to hear this. He was not looking forward to leaving Augg behind and none of the women wanted to volunteer to stay with him. They all wanted to go to the rendezvous. Dearth was glad that Augg changed his mind for he knew it would end up causing hurt feelings if a woman was forced to stay behind with him. He also felt it might help Augg if he got to go and see other people. It might even help take his mind off his heartache.

The men have built five new travois. On them, they have loaded enough long wooden poles and hides to build three shelters for them to stay in while they are there. On the other travois, they have put the things they hope to trade, which are more hides and a few spear tips. For Augg's comfort, he will be placed on one of the travois atop some hides that they are bringing along to trade.

It is a three-day walk to reach the spot where Drog told Dearth the rendezvous is to be held. Dearth decides to leave one day early just to make sure he can find it and make the trip easier on Augg and those pulling him.

As the men pack the last things onto the travois, Ock and Gogg help Augg out to one of them and sit him down on top of a pile of bison hides. They know he deserves their respect and they would want the clan to treat them the same if anything ever happened to them. After Augg is lying on the travois, they place a folded-up deer hide under his head for a pillow. "Augg want cover?" Ock asked.

Augg shakes his head. "I good," he said, looking at them and grinning.

The two young men then go to the front of the travois, lift the poles, and are ready to go. Everyone is all smiles as they head off to the west to find the rendezvous place. They are all anxious to meet the other clans in the area.

On the way there, Ock and Gogg talk about the possibility of finding a woman they can join with. Ock is already nineteen-years-old and Gogg is seventeen. Both are more than ready to be joined with a woman and can hardly wait to see if there are any young women at the rendezvous that are attractive *and* that are available.

Dearth and his clan arrive at the place Drog told them of a day early and there are already nearly fifty people there. Someone has built a fire in the center of six temporary shelters. Around the fire are several men and women along with a half dozen children that are running and playing. It only takes Dearth a moment to spot Drog and when he does, Drog looks up at him and grins. Drog then walks over to meet him. "Drog happy to see leader Dearth. Come, sit by fire, rest," Drog said, as he looks at all of those that are with Dearth.

The others nod and greet him with a smile as they all head toward center of the camp.

After Dearth's clan arrives, the men go to work erecting the three shelters next to the others that are already there. While Ock and Gogg are unloading the poles, they look to see two young women come out of one of the shelters across from them. Both are attractive and when the girls see the two young men, they look up and smile. The men know that if these girls were already married, they would never smile at them, so their hopes of finding a mate has just risen to great heights.

Ock and Gogg rush to finish their job so they can find out who these two girls are. Before they are even finished, however, the two girls come over to Drog and begin talking to him. Ock drops everything as does Gogg and they walk over to find out about the girls.

When they come up to Drog, the girls see them approaching and again look up and smile. Ock and Gogg smile back as they step up beside Drog.

Ock is the boldest and he looks at the girls and then over at Drog. "Drog have daughters?" he asked.

Drog sees the young men's interest in the girls and gives them his toothless grin. "Daughters not mine," he replied, and both boys' hearts sank. "Girls orphans in Drog's clan."

The boys' spirits soar again. "Girls not joined?" Ock asked.

Drog's eyes sparkle as he sees how much these two young men want the girls and how much the girls are interested. "Girls not joined. Looking for man soon," he said, studying the boys' reaction.

Ock cannot hide his enthusiasms as he shuffles from one foot then to another trying not to show how interested he is. While he is talking with Drog, the girls start whispering to one another and giggling, as they are looking over at Ock and Gogg.

"We not joined with woman," Gogg said. "We like to make trade."

Ock looks over at Gogg and gives him a stern look letting him know he shouldn't show too much interest right off. In trading, never let the other person know how much you want something or the price will go higher. You should play it down and act as though you could take it or leave it.

Drog knows he has the boys' complete attention. The boys, too, know that he does and at this moment they would give everything they have to be joined with these girls because both are stunning.

Drog looks the boys in the eyes, then looks over at the girls, and then back at the boys again. "Drog talk with leader Dearth. See if he wants to trade."

Ock and Gogg smile. "We go speak with Dearth," Ock said. "Tell him you have two women to trade."

Drog grins again as the boys walk over to where Dearth is sitting resting. Before the boys are there, Dearth already knows what they are coming to see him about for he has been watching the entire thing.

When Ock and Gogg come near, Dearth acts as if he does not know anything. Ock is the one to step forward. "Dearth," Ock said, "Drog has two girls."

Gogg jumps in, "Both are orphans and he said he might trade them to us for wives."

Dearth seems surprised. "Wives?" he asked, looking at their faces and seeing they are waiting in anticipation for what he is going to say. "Do girls look good?"

Ock nods. "Girls look good," he answered, with a big smile on his face.

Gogg nods in agreement.

"What girls' names?" Dearth asked.

Ock seems to be caught off guard. "Not know. Just see them. No talk to them."

Gogg nods again.

Dearth smiles and gets up from the log he is sitting on. "I go see about girls," he said with a half grin.

Ock and Gogg both grin from ear to ear as Dearth goes over to speak with Drog.

Drog has been keeping an eye on both Ock and Gogg and knows they are anxious to have the girls as wives. He also sees that the girls seem just as anxious to have the boys as husbands. The girls are still talking and giggling as they sit nearby watching the entire scene play out.

When Dearth comes near, he looks over at the two girls and sees that they are indeed attractive. Drog steps forward to meet him and gives him his snaggle-toothed grin. "Boys want to make trade for girls," he said.

Dearth nods and smiles. "Boys young, always want girl. I tell them I see if girls are good for wives," Dearth said, looking over at them once more.

"Girls good," Drog said. "Never been joined to man. Right age to be wives."

Dearth looks into Drog's eyes. "Why Drog want to trade girls?"

Drog looks down at the ground then back up to Dearth, then over at the girls. "Girls orphans. Orphans since father killed by cave bear and mother die of sickness."

"Girls sisters?" Dearth asked.

Drog nods and replies, "No man to help feed them. Clan go hungry sometimes."

Dearth understands that Drog is anxious to get rid of extra mouths to feed. That was one reason he wanted the

119

leftovers of the rhino Dearth and his men had killed that day. He also knows Drog will trade whatever he can get for the girls.

"Dearth think we can trade," Dearth said. "What want?"

Drog has already learned to trust Dearth. Dearth showed him kindness when he let Drog have the meat when he and his clan were going hungry. He will not try and take advantage of him. "Whatever leader Dearth says is good trade," Drog answered.

Dearth nods and looks over at the girls once again. "What girls' names?"

"Young one, Mursa. Mursa thirteen summers. Other girl, Ee'ga," Drog answers. "Ee'ga fifteen summers."

Dearth seems pleased and looks back at Drog. Dearth then nods. "Good age for joining. "Drog take three bison hides and two bags jerky for each?" Dearth asked, holding up his fingers for emphasis.

Drog grins as he looks up at Dearth's face. "Good trade for girls. Girls make good wives for Dearth's clan."

Dearth nods in agreement and puts forth his right arm. Drog reaches out, clasps Dearth's upper forearm and the men shake on the deal.

Dearth smiles and puts his hand on Drog's shoulder. "Trade good. I go tell Ock, Gogg, to come back with hides and meat for trade."

Drog nods and watches Dearth walk back toward the boys. As soon as Dearth walks away, the girls run up to Drog. "Drog make trade?" Ee'ga asked.

Drog nods and sees the joy on their faces.

When Dearth returns to Ock and Gogg, he is somber faced and the boys do not know if he has made a deal or not. Ock studies his face for any signs that the deal went through. He can wait no longer. The tension is mounting in his body, so Ock anxiously blurts out, "Trade for girls?"

Dearth looks at him then over at Gogg. He then cracks a huge smile. "No worry. Dearth trade."

Ock and Gogg's face lights up. "Trade for both girls?" Gogg asked, thinking he might be left out. It is customary for the oldest boy to get the first choice of a bride in situations such as this.

"Dearth trade for both Ee'ga and Mursa," Dearth replied.

"Which one oldest?" Ock asked, hoping the one he has his eye will be his.

"Ee'ga fifteen summers old. Mursa thirteen summers."

Ock is very pleased. Gogg also has no problem with Mursa for she is pretty, too.

"What Dearth trade?" Ock asked.

"Three bison hides for each girl and two bags of bison jerky for each."

"We get hides and meat and trade now?" Gogg asked.

Dearth sees the boys are very impatient, so he gives them a nod. The two young men rush to get the hides from one of the travois and the jerky from another. In a couple of minutes, they return with their arms full. "We go now and trade?" Ock asked.

Dearth nods and grins. "Go make trade."

The boys hurry over to Drog who is standing waiting where Dearth left him. The girls are still sitting nearby smiling as they watch Ock and Gogg hurry over.

Drog looks pleased as he sees the bison hides and points to the shelter where the girls are sitting. "Put hides inside," he said, as the boys near.

Ock and Gogg take them over and cram the hides through the small opening then quickly return to Drog. "Hides and meat inside," Gogg said.

Drog looks over at the girls and nods. "Go with young men. You belong to leader Dearth's clan now."

The girls jump to their feet and rush over to Ock and Gogg. All four are smiling. Ock looks at Ee'ga. "Ock take Ee'ga."

Gogg looks at Mursa. "Gogg take Mursa."

The girls then follow them over to their camp. When they come back to Dearth, Ock and Gogg motion for Dearth to step away from the girls so they can ask him a question. Once they are several steps away, Ock turns to Dearth. "Can we be joined with wives today?"

Dearth grins and glances back at the girls who are smiling and watching him. "Do girls want to be joined?"

Ock nods and smiles. "Ee'ga want to be joined today."

Gogg jumps in. "Mursa want to be joined to Gogg today, too."

Dearth grins again and looks at Ock's and Gogg's faces that are beaming. How can he turn them down? Ock is already nineteen and he has been wanting to find a mate for the last three years. "Dearth do joining at sunset tomorrow after everyone here. Get to know girls better by then."

Ock and Gogg nod then run over to tell their brides-to-be that they will be joined tomorrow at sunset. All four of them are full of joy and anticipation and can hardly wait to become wives.

During the day, several more clans come and set up temporary shelters and mingle with one another. The following day, a few more clans show up.

After everyone that is coming has arrived, Dearth announces the joining ceremony of Ock and Gogg to Ee'ga and Mursa. Right after he makes the announcement, three other clan leaders come forth and ask him if he would join couples in their clan at the same time. They had also found one another at the rendezvous. Dearth tells them he would be honored.

Chapter 28

The Great Joining Ceremony

There is great excitement all throughout the many clans that are there. No one has ever seen five couples joined at the same time. By late that afternoon, the women in the other clans are already busy working to get the brides ready.

As the women in Dearth's clan help Ee'ga and Mursa prepare for their joining, Ock and Gogg, too, are getting prepared for the great ceremony. They have put on their best clothing, have their favorite spear close by and have their faces and arms painted with red ocher. They have also put on a necklace made of cave bear claws and fangs of a saber-tooth tiger.

The three leaders, which asked Dearth to join their couples, ask him to explain how he will perform the ceremony, because each clan does it a little differently. After he gives them the details, they are well pleased. Each leader then leaves to tell the men and women of their respective clans how the five-couple joining ceremony will be done.

When Drog hears about the joining ceremony, he comes over to Dearth's shelter. When Dearth sees him approaching carrying one of the bison skins he had traded for the young women, he is surprised.

When Drog steps up beside him, he is grinning and Dearth is looking at him, trying to figure out why he is bringing the hide back. "Hide not good?" Dearth asked.

"Hide good," Drog replied, nodding. "Want give two hides to Ee'ga and Mursa for joining."

Dearth smiles. "Good gift. Will Drog take two pieces of roasted bison meat as gift?"

Drog nods and smiles from ear to ear. "Drog take meat. Be back with other hide."

Dearth takes the hide from Drog, puts it in the shelter and then goes to get the meat. Meanwhile, Drog goes and retrieves the second bison hide and brings it back. After they take one another gifts they get busy preparing for the ceremony.

Crug happens to be nearby when he sees Drog bringing the hide over to Dearth. He and his brother, Bogg, had been away from camp and hadn't heard about Ock and Gogg finding the girls or the trade that Dearth had made. Coming over to Dearth after Drog leaves, Crug stops and stares at Dearth, who is bent over folding the bison robe. "What trade for?" he asked.

Dearth rises up and sees Crug standing their waiting for an answer. "Dearth trade for two girls for Ock and Gogg."

Crug is confused. "If Dearth trade for girls, why Drog bring hide and you give meat?"

"I trade three hides for each girl and some meat. Drog give back one hide for each girl for joining today. I give Drog more meat."

Crug is enraged. "Drog would pay Dearth to take girls. He can no feed them."

"I make fair trade," Dearth said.

"Dearth not know fair trade," Crug said. He then storms off in a huff.

After the women in Dearth's clan are dressed in their best clothing, have their necklaces on and the red ocher on their faces, they are waiting for Dearth to begin. The men and women in the other clans are also ready and everyone is gathering near the fire in the center of the camp.

When the five grooms step out of the shelters, everyone turns to look. They come forward and stand in front of Dearth with smiles on each of their faces, as they wait for their brides to make their appearance. Just inside their separate shelters, the girls are watching the grooms. They are peeking out from behind the bison hides that cover the entrances to make sure all five of them step out at the same time.

Then, as the grooms and everyone else is looking toward the shelters, the brides come out and meet in the center of the camp. Once they are side-by-side, they start walking toward Dearth and the grooms. When they come near Dearth, they break apart and each girl goes over to her groom and stands on his left side. They smile and look at Dearth.

Ock and Gogg look down the row of brides and see that their brides are much prettier than the other three. Ee'ga and Mursa both have on a hip hugging buckskin skirt that shows off their curves. Neither can the buckskin top they are wearing hide their bountiful breasts.

The sun is just beginning to set as Dearth looks at all the soon-to-be newlyweds standing before him. Ock and Gogg are happy but a little apprehensive. They will now have much more responsibility. They not only will have to take care of themselves but a wife, and after that, there will be children to care for as well.

The girls don't seem to be so apprehensive and are all smiles. As they are standing there waiting, Ee'ga reaches over and takes Ock's hand and squeezes it to let him know she is happy. Ock looks at her, shakes his head and whispers, "Woman not to hold man's hand till Dearth tell her."

She smiles and releases her grip, then wipes the sweat from her palm on her clothing; the sweat she got from Ock's sweaty hand.

Everyone there has gathered around so as to not miss a single thing. Even the children are curious as to what is happening. Roosa is standing nearby with several small pieces of roasted bison meat that she will present to Dearth at the appropriate times. The men have their spears resting on the ground on their right side with the tip pointing into the air.

Dearth looks at each bride and groom. "Now you will be man and woman together," he said, taking his open hands and entwining his fingers. Then closing his hands together, which symbolizes the joining between the two, he looks at all the couples again. After this, he reaches over, takes Ee'ga's right hand and places it in Oct's left hand. Next, he does the same ritual to Gogg and Mursa, then to the other three couples.

Glancing behind him, Dearth looks at Roosa and nods. She steps forward with ten small pieces of the roasted bison meat. She must use two hands to hold them and reaching out, she opens her hands to Dearth. He takes one of the pieces and then turns to Ock. Taking the piece of meat, he hands it to Ock; he then then places it between his lips. Next, Ock turns his head, looks at Ee'ga and leans forward, so she can take the meat from him with her lips.

Gently, Ee'ga takes the meat from Ock's lips and slowly she begins chewing it. This means she has accepted Ock as her mate and her provider.

Roosa then hands Dearth a second piece of meat and he himself places it between Ee'ga's lips. She leans forward toward Ock; he then takes the meat from between her lips and begins to chew it slowly. This symbolizes that she will help her husband and take care of all his needs.

After this, Dearth walks over and picks up one of the large bison robes that Drog gave for Ee'ga's and Mursa's joining. Coming back over to the couple, he wraps it around both of them. Being wrapped together in a cocoon of skin signifies that they are now and will forever be together as a couple.

Dearth does the same thing with Gogg and Mursa. Afterward, he wraps them in the other robe that Drog gave him. He then continues and does the same for the other three couples. Once he has finished this, Dearth steps forward and hugs each couple that is wrapped together. They are now joined. At this, all the other members of all the clans that are there begin shouting and dancing. This is the end of the joining ceremony. The couples are now joined and will be until one of them dies.

After the ceremony, the dancing and celebrating continue well into the night. Everyone is happy for the couples. While the celebrating is going on, Ock and Gogg slip away with their new brides, and crawl under the animal skins where they typically would sleep. None of the five couples will be getting much sleep tonight; they will be celebrating in a different way.

Outside, the women in Dearth's clan are smiling, knowing that Ee'ga and Mursa will become one with their husbands tonight. The brides are also anxious to know how it feels to be a woman with a man as they have heard stories of how great it is from the married women. Ock and Gogg are even more anxious to please their wives and enjoy being a man and a husband. It will be a night none of them will ever forget.

After the joining of the five couples, the clans stay for three days and nights. In the middle of the camp they have several large fires burning night and day where they roast fresh meat they have brought along. They also celebrate at night with dancing, beating of log drums and telling exciting stories of past hunts. It is a time that none of them will forget, especially Ock and Gogg.

Chapter 29

The Birth of Mulda

After the festivities of the rendezvous, the clan members have returned home at the cave and settled into daily life once again. During all the excitement at the rendezvous, Ulda had mostly forgotten about her prior pregnancy troubles. After a miscarriage and a baby that died shortly after birth, she is worried that she will lose this baby, too. So far, Ulda's pregnancy has been normal and her delivery day is fast approaching. Now that there is nothing else to occupy her mind, she begins to focus on the upcoming birth of the baby that is currently kicking inside of her.

It is early morning and her husband, Durr, has already gotten up and gone outside when her labor pains begin. The first person she tells is Roosa, as she will help with the delivery. Roosa is very happy for her and tries to calm her fears. "Baby be good this time," Roosa said. "Be strong baby. Live to be very old."

Ulda smiles and hopes she is right. "I go tell Durr," Ulda said.

Roosa looks at her and smiles. "Durr be happy. Go tell husband and Roosa help with baby."

Ulda then goes outside to find him. Upon exiting the cave, she sees Durr sitting outside with the other men talking. The men that are facing the cave entrance stop talking when they see her coming. Durr turns to see what they are looking at and sees a grimace on Ulda's face then notices that she has her hands on her swollen belly. From these actions he figures she is having labor pains. "Time for baby?" he asked, standing to his feet.

Ulda nods and gives him a slight smile. Durr can also tell she is nervous. "Go inside," Durr said, getting up and coming over to her. They then walk back into the cave and go to the area where the birthing rocks are.

When they leave, the men begin talking again, this time about the baby that is coming. Soon everyone is talking and excited that a new clan member is to arrive shortly. Ulda is in labor all day and by nightfall, her pains are very close together. Roosa knows the baby is about ready to be born.

Ulda is squatted down between the rocks in front of two bison hides and Dearth's wife, Ursa, is there wiping the sweat from her brow. Roosa is in front waiting and watching for the head of the baby to appear, when Ulda has another hard contraction. "There is head!" Roosa exclaimed. "One more push and baby be here."

A few seconds after this contraction, Ulda has another and Roosa has the infant in her hands. The baby is red, wrinkled and squirming, as Roosa uses her teeth to bite the umbilical cord in two.

Ulda looks over, sees that it is a girl and smiles. She then leans back and Ursa helps her to lie down on the bison hides and rest.

Durr is standing nearby and when he sees the baby in Roosa's hands, he comes over to her to see what sex it is. When he sees that it is a girl, he looks over at Ulda. "Baby girl like Ulda want."

Ulda smiles. "Baby girl name Mulda."

"Mulda good name," Roosa said. "Baby strong. Live to be old woman."

Ulda and Durr couldn't be any happier. Ulda has finally gotten a baby and this time a healthy one. Mulda will indeed live to be old and she will be a blessing to her clan, but that is another story.

Chapter 30

A Year Later

One year after Mulda is born, she is still healthy and is already trying to walk. Ulda and Durr are the happiest they have ever been.

It seems the only one that is not happy is Crug. He obeys Dearth's orders but everyone can see his resentment. They know it is just a matter of time before there will be a confrontation between them.

Game has been plentiful and the clan is prospering as never before. There has been a new clan that has moved in from the far south. Dearth and his men have only met them from a distance. When they saw them, the strangers did not raise their spears in peace, so Dearth decided not to introduce himself. It seems there is always a bad neighbor that thinks they are better than anyone else.

The new neighbors have also proven to be thieves. After killing a bison recently, Dearth and his hunting party butchered it and carried as much meat as they could back to the cave. When they returned to the carcass to finish their job, they found that someone had been there and had taken every last piece of meat. It was evident that it wasn't scavengers because Dearth could see that the meat had been cut from the bones with a flint knife. The only ones he knew that could have done it were the new neighbors. They must have followed Dearth's hunting party and after they made a kill, came and stole the meat.

Crug wanted to go and kill the men of the clan but Dearth said no. He said it wasn't worth one of his clansmen to die over a few pounds of meat. This only made Crug resent Dearth even more. He said if he was the leader, he would kill every last member of the new clan.

Chapter 31

The Accident

The following spring, the herds of bison are heading north and Dearth decides the clan should follow them. They pack three travois with poles and hides for temporary shelters and two others will be for food and weapons. One other travois is made for carrying Augg. Dearth and Ock will be dragging him while Gogg and Mooth drag one of the heavier ones that is loaded with food and weapons. Durr drags one of the lighter ones and the women will take turns dragging the others.

Mulda is only two-years-old at this time and she will sometimes ride with Augg and at other times with four-year-old Braum when he gets too tired to walk. The clan will spend all summer going north and returning with the herds in the fall.

As they prepare to leave, everyone is excited to have a change of scenery. It has been a long cold winter and they are tired of being confined to the dreary cave most of the time. It will be a pleasant break to see green grass and breathe fresh air.

Mulda does not seem anxious to go and when Ulda puts her on the travois, she begins crying. Braum sees her, shakes his head thinking she is just a girl and has no idea of the thrill it is to be heading into the wilderness. Braum is full of joy to be going on this adventure. The men will be hunting and if he is lucky, he might get to see them kill a bison or even a mammoth.

After Augg takes his place on the travois, he looks over at Mulda who is still upset about the trip. "Bring Mulda," he said, reaching his arms out.

Ulda picks her up, takes her over to Augg and sets her down between his legs so he can hold her. "Mulda be good girl," he said, putting his big hands around her waist to keep her from getting up. "Stay here with Augg," he said, smiling. "We get to ride."

Little Mulda looks up at his whiskered covered face and stops pouting.

Augg pats her back and looks to see Dearth and Ock come out of the cave. Dearth stops beside Augg and sees that he has Mulda. "Ready to go?" he asked.

Augg grins. "We all ready."

Dearth then walks to the front of the travois along with Ock and they lift it up and start pulling it across the ground. The others also take hold of their travois and follow him. Braum is walking behind then runs up to the front with his father, Dearth. "You kill great beast soon?" he asked.

Dearth looks down into his son's brown eyes. "Not know. Kill great beast, kill bison, kill other animal."

"Braum hope your kill great beast. Braum want see great beast fall from spear."

Dearth smiles. "Braum get to see plenty great beasts. Someday hunt great beasts."

Braum sure hopes so and he can hardly wait until he is old enough to go on hunts with his father.

For several days, they travel north but only see a few scattered bison. On the fourth day, near sunset, they find a large herd of several thousand bison along a river. When Dearth and the men see the big herd, they stop near the riverbank. "We camp here," Dearth said, and everyone sets down their travois and begins unloading the poles for the shelters.

Early the following morning, the men are up early and then are soon on their way toward the bison herd. They are taking along the wolf skins, so they can put them on their backs and crawl on their hands and knees to get close to the animals.

The herd is still along the river where they were last night, which is about a quarter of a mile upstream. When the men get within about two hundred yards, they stop and tie the wolf hides on one another's backs. They then drop down onto their hands and knees. Reaching up, they pull the wolf's head over their own so they will appear to be a small pack of wolves on the hunt.

The herd is busy grazing as the men close the gap. They are still slowing crawling on their hands and knees with a spear clutched in each hand. When they are about fifty yards away, a big bull bison sees them and turns to face the men or wolves as the bison thinks. When Dearth and the others see him turn to face them, they clutch the two spears tighter in their hands and continue advancing toward the herd.

A few yards further and the bison snorts, which gets the attention of several others nearby and they, too, turn to face what they think are wolves. Dearth is out front and when he is within about twenty yards, the big bull charges straight at him. When it gets close and sees that the wolf does not run it stops. Right then, Dearth jumps to his feet as do the other men and prepare to launch their spears. The bison is surprised that the wolves have suddenly disappeared and now men are standing in their place. He turns to run and this is when Dearth and the others throw their spears, which sink deep into the bison's ribcage.

The massive bull takes off running at top speed and this causes the others near him to also run away. The men are in no hurry to pursue him because he must die from blood loss, which may take several minutes or even several hours. They will watch and wait; keeping an eye on him and following close behind, but not close enough to make him keep running.

Back at camp, Braum is standing on his tiptoes trying to see the men and the bison. The women, too, are watching. They are fascinated how the men can get so close to a wild bison, and how brave they are.

Augg is still asleep and while everyone's attention is on the men, little Mulda comes out of her mother's shelter and heads for the river. She is nearly to the bank before Braum sees her out the corner of his eye and turns around. Fear grips his heart as he watches her toddling toward the step bank. "No!" he screams and, in a flash, he runs as fast as he can to reach her.

Ulda and the other women hear Braum yell and turn around to see what is happening. Ulda is terrified as she screams and runs toward the river.

When Braum nears the bank, he sees Mulda step over the edge and disappear from sight. A few seconds later, he is at the bank's edge and looks down to see her tumble into the swift water, then go under. With a big leap, he jumps down to the water's edge where he can see her just under the surface. Rushing into the ice-cold water, he reaches down, takes hold of her arm and pulls her out so she can breathe.

By this time, Ulda is at the top of the bank with the other women right behind her. Ulda is screaming and crying as she stumbles down the bank to get to her baby. Braum sees her coming and holds Mulda up, so her mother can take her. The other women, except for Roosa, climb down to the water's edge and help get Ulda and her baby back up the bank.

Once on top, Ursa sees that the Mulda is coughing but breathing. "Baby be good. Cold and wet, but alive," Roosa said. "Take off wet clothes and wrap baby in dry clothes."

Ulda hurries to the shelter to wrap Mulda in some dry warm skins and to hold her close until she knows she is all right. It was a close call but she will be fine.

When Dearth and his hunting party return later that day, they are told of Braum's heroic action that saved little Mulda. Dearth and Ursa could not be any prouder of him. This is the first of many heroic actions that Braum will achieve in his life.

Chapter 32

Crug's Anger

Winter passes without incident and nothing very exciting happens to the clan by the time spring arrives the following year, but that will soon change. Mulda is now three and Braum is five. Oddly enough, none of the women are pregnant and thankfully no one has died. Mooth has turned eleven and is looking forward to when he can go on mammoth hunts with the men. The clan settles into a routine and life goes on from one day to the next in the usual fashion.

As soon as the weather breaks and spring arrives for good, Dearth is planning on taking the clan on their usual hunting trip north to follow the herds of bison, reindeer and mammoths. Crug, however, thinks they should head northwest this year into new territory.

When he brings this up, everyone is sitting around the fire one night just outside the cave. "Why Dearth go north again?" Crug asked. "Go to new land and hunt."

"Plenty of game where clan always go," Dearth said. "New land have other clans that hunt. No want to kill game other clans hunt. Plenty where we hunt."

Crug is angry. He still has much resentment for Dearth being made clan leader by Crug's younger brother Brock. He already had resentment for their father making Brock the leader. He is the oldest of their father's sons and he thought the honor of being leader should have been his. He feels cheated that the leadership role was stolen from him. Because of this, it seems he always wants to cause conflict and this rubs Dearth the wrong way. Dearth does the best he can and cares for the welfare of the *entire* clan.

Crug does not care so much for the clan as he does for himself. If Dearth was to go where Crug wanted, another clan might think they were trying to take over the area and start a fight with Dearth's clan. Maybe something might happen to Dearth. He could even die. Then Crug could be leader.

Dearth wants to live in peace with his neighbors, especially the ones that have proven to be good neighbors. He sees no reason to change their hunting plans or to possibly borrow trouble when things have been fine the way they are.

"We go *north*," Dearth asserts, while looking Crug directly in the eyes, "above Great River and hunt."

Crug jumps up from the log he is sitting on and storms off into the darkness. Once he is out of sight, Ock turns to Dearth. "Crug still angry he not leader."

Dearth nods. "Brock was good leader. He know Crug be bad leader."

Ock agrees, but this will not be the end of it. Crug has this stuck in his craw and he cannot get over the fact his father and his brother chose others over him.

Chapter 33

The Night of Rumbling

After Crug got over his temper tantrum, he went along with Dearth and the rest of the clan north. After they built some rafts and went across The Great River, as they call it, they made camp for the evening. They have brought along several travois, which carry their supplies of meat, weapons and building materials for the shelters they will use for the summer months.

Dearth has chosen a spot near the riverbank but there is no wood for a fire. They have some small kindling to start one but there are no trees nearby to gather wood to keep a fire going. The nearest trees are several miles away and they cannot reach the area before nightfall. That is the reason Dearth has made camp here. Because of this, they will have a cold camp tonight.

Crug is not happy with that fact and he is sulking. He thinks he would be a much better leader and if they would have gone where he wanted to go, they would have a warm fire tonight and some hot food. Crug detests jerky.

Soon after turning in for the night, everyone falls fast asleep. Then, just before daybreak, Dearth is awakened by a deep rumbling sound. He can feel the ground trembling beneath him and the sound seems to be getting louder. At first, he thinks it is thunder in the distance but thunder is loud then dies down. This sound is getting louder and then it hits him: *it's a stampede!*

Throwing off his cover of a heavy bison skin, Dearth jumps to his feet. "Wake up!" he shouts. "Get to river! Stampede coming!"

Everyone in all three shelters hears him yelling and they scramble to their feet still half asleep. Ursa grabs Braum and Ulda picks up Mulda in her arms. Ock is in another shelter, he helps Augg to his feet, and they all hurry outside.

When they step out into the darkness, Crug and the others have also come outside and they all hear the hoof beats of the approaching animals. The thunderous sound is almost deafening as they hurry down to the water's edge. Just as they step into the frigid river, they see what it is. Hundreds of frightened bison are running along the river heading upstream. Seconds later, they run right toward the three shelters, and as the people stand there in the river, they see the shelters get toppled over and stomped on by the big shaggy beasts. If they would have been inside, they would have been trampled to death!

It takes a good three minutes for all the animals to pass by. When Dearth sees the last one go by, he steps out of the river and walks up the bank. It is just light enough to see some of the damage. All three shelters have been trampled on and it looks as if some of the poles are broken. The bison hides that covered them are dirty but usable. The water bags have been stepped on, too, but can be refilled.

By now, Ock and Gogg are coming up beside Dearth and begin to search through the trampled travois looking for their spears. Ock soon finds them. When he pulls them out, he finds most are broken, but a few are still intact. It will be a lot of work but everything can be replaced as soon as they get to a forest.

As the men are picking up the pieces, Braum comes over to Dearth, who is bent over one the travois trying to find their jerky and roasted meat. "What cause bison to run?" Braum asked, looking at his father.

Dearth pulls out a bag of jerky and looks up. "Not know. Spear cat maybe. Wolves attack. Never know."

By now, the women have gathered around trying to find their clothes in the crushed shelters. They need to change Braum, Mulda and themselves into some dry clothing to take away the chills they are having from being in the cold water of the river.

Crug and his wife, Ni'na, are sifting through their belongings and everyone can hear Crug grumbling that this wouldn't have happened if they had gone where he wanted to go.

A few days later, everything has been repaired and the summer goes without any more trouble. This, however, is just the calm before the storm, as troubled days are yet ahead.

Chapter 34

The Sickness

Another year has passed. Mulda has now just turned four and Braum is six. It is nearing spring again and to those living in the cave; it has been a long and boring winter. The little ones were beginning to get on everyone's nerves.

No one in the clan has been sick for quite a long time. There have been a few scrapes and bruises, but nothing serious. There were some very minor injuries the men got while hunting and others occurred when the children got to playing a bit too rambunctious. Other than that, no one has fallen ill for many months.

It seems things cannot go well for very long, however, before trouble comes along and this was the case for this clan. One morning as everyone is getting up to start their day, Braum and Mulda both are found to be running a fever. Roosa is the only one that has any knowledge when it comes to healing, so the mothers call on her to look at them. At first, she thinks it could have been something they ate because soon after waking they got sick at their stomach and began vomiting.

Ursa makes some hot broth with some bison meat and tries to get them to eat a little. They take a few bites but throw it right back up as soon as it hits their stomach. They then begin to have chills.

Roosa and Ursa have them to lie down side-by-side and cover them with two heavy bison hides. This keeps them warm and soon they begin to sweat.

"Sweat good," Roosa said. "Sweat out fever."

Their fever does break by the next morning, but they have diarrhea for two more days. Finally, they are able to keep some food down and start getting better. No one ever knew what it was that made them ill, but Roosa still thought it was something they ate. The Neanderthals knew nothing of germs and neither would anyone else for tens of thousands of years.

After the children's sickness, things go pretty smooth until the following year. This will be the year that changes the lives of every clan member and none of them will never be the same again.

Chapter 35

The Great Beast

It is early the following year and the eleven-man hunting party has just spotted a small herd of woolly mammoths feeding near a river. The men are sneaking up along the river's edge using the bushes for cover. They must work together to bring down what they call the "great beast", which is a fifteen to twenty-ton behemoth that can crush them like an ant if they make a mistake.

Along on his first mammoth hunt is thirteen-year-old Mooth. Dearth didn't really want him to come because of the danger but Mooth persisted in asking and Dearth finally gave in. With Augg no longer able to go on hunts, they can certainly use his eyes if nothing else.

It is mating season for the mammoths and a huge bull is in musts. His testosterone level is the highest it's been all year and he is a little more than angry, he is enraged. His anger stems from the fact that there is another large bull that wants to move in on his cows. The new bull soon challenges the older bull and a fight quickly ensues. The huge bulls look at one another to size each other up. Then, with anger in their eyes they rush forward, locking tusks and trunks. As they begin shoving one another, trying to see who can get the upper hand, the ground around them is churned up with dirt and grass flying in all directions. The cows, however, pay little mind to the titanic struggle going on nearby. It's no real concern to them which male wins. The cows will only mate if they are in season and only a few of them are.

The men have been waiting for this opportunity. While the bulls are fighting, they will not be focused on anything else. They will not even see the men that are coming closer.

Dearth looks back at those in the hunting party and motions for them to go along the river. This way, if one of the herd charges, they can dive into the river and have a better change of escaping. Dearth sneaks down to the water's edge and begins going along the shore using the bushes there to conceal himself and those following him.

Unknown to him, however, Crug has motioned for some of the men to follow him. They are going along the other side of the bushes several yards from the river. With him is his son, Brant, his brother Bogg, Nagar, Graun, Durock and Durr.

Dearth is focused on the two mammoths fighting and doesn't look back at those men with him. Once he is close enough, he readies his spear, as do the men behind him. They creep forward and prepare to launch them at the nearest bull. "Now!" Dearth yells, and the men throw their spears with all their strength.

The men on the other side of the bushes with Crug also throw their spears and all eleven spears strike the huge bull. Some hit him in his left ribcage and others hit him in the neck and right rib cage. A couple of the spears hit the rib bones and do not penetrate very deeply. The others, however, go between the ribs and sink very deep, puncturing at least one of the bull's lungs.

Upon impact, the bull that has been hit, breaks off his challenge with the other bull and turns toward the men that are on the far side of the bushes with Crug. He is now even angrier. He couldn't defeat the other bull but he can take out his anger on the puny men that have dared to try and kill him. When the massive bull turns to face the men, he flares out his ears and lifts his trunk giving a spine-chilling trumpet. The enormous bull then charges, determined to kill his adversaries.

Dearth and those with him see what is happening, but there is little they can do except throw their second spear and try to stop the attack. With only seconds before the bull is on the other men, Dearth, Ock, Mooth and Gogg throw their spears. Only two hit him solid because he is running and the two that do, do not slow him down in the least.

The men with Crug can see the anger in the bull's eyes as he barrels down on them. They do not run, however, but take hold of their last spear and stand their ground. When the raging bull is only a few yards away, they launch their second spears and every one of them hits the charging animal.

He does not stop or slow down, however, but keeps coming. The men then jump to the side and try to get out of his way. Crug, Bogg, Durock, along with Durr manage to dive into the bushes just in time. The other three men, Graun, Nagar and Brant are not so lucky. The enraged animal knocks one after another down to the ground. First, his attention is focused on Brant. Using his trunk, he holds the helpless man in place and lowers his enormous head down onto his body, crushing him beneath. The men can hear bones being broken as Brant's life is extinguished.

No sooner has the mammoth killed Brant, he looks over at Graun, who is trying to get up and run. But before Graun can get to his feet, the mammoth sees him, rushes over with his ears flared, trunk and tail raised and does the same to him.

Nagar is still lying on the ground for he was nearly rendered unconscious when the mammoth ran over him and knocked him down. He tries to get up but before he can, the mammoth sees him moving and turns around towards him. Again, he flares out his ears and charges the already injured man. Then, using his head as a battering ram, he drives Nagar into the ground, snuffing out his life.

There is nothing the other men can do but watch. After the attack, the mammoth stops, looks around, then slowly walks off. He is feeling weak by this time, as he has lost a lot of blood. He doesn't get far before the blood in his lungs drowns him, and he falls over and cannot get up.

Crug, Gogg and Durr are the first to reach their fallen comrades, but the men are already dead. Dearth and those with him walk up and stand beside Crug, who is kneeling over his youngest brother, Brant. Brant was just thirty-two-years old. Graun was but twenty-eight and Nagar was forty-eight. All leave wives behind and they will be devastated. Nagar was too old to even be along but he wanted to go and help. Now he leaves Roosa behind and she will have to live the rest of her life alone.

Crug looks up at Dearth with sadness in his eyes. Dearth is more angry than sad at this moment. "Why not listen when Dearth say go along river?" Dearth asked.

Crug's sadness now turns to anger and he jumps to his feet, looking Dearth in the eyes. "Why men listen to Dearth. If all men follow Crug, men kill great beast and men not die."

This makes Dearth furious. Ever since Brock became clan leader Crug as has harbored resentment. When Brock made Dearth leader his resentment only grew.

"Dearth leader of clan!" Dearth growls, his face flushed with anger. "Crug killed men! Crug not follow us along river. If Crug and men listen to Dearth, could go in river, hide from great beast and not die. Now men dead! Cannot bring men back to life!"

Crug is so mad that he turns and walks away, but then comes back and looks at Dearth again. "Crug not follow Dearth no more! Crug leave and be leader of own clan!"

Dearth nods. "Crug leave. Take all people that want to follow Crug. Dearth stay and others stay with Dearth."

Crug nods and walks away. There will be some that leave with him and some that stay. This will be a test and it will split the clan in two! It is a sad day and a day that will have numerous repercussions.

Chapter 36

The Split

Dearth and the men with him have stayed behind. They begin work to make three travois. It will take them several hours to complete their work. Three hours later, they are done and place the bodies of the three dead men on them. The hunting party will come back later and butcher the mammoth they killed, but now they need to get the bodies back home and bury them.

When Crug returns to the cave, everyone inside can see something is very wrong. Roosa is the first to notice Crug when he enters and sees the anger on his face. Bogg and Durr are with him but not her husband, Nagar.

When she sees the men enter without her husband, her heart sinks. Kuma and Sora also do not see their husbands and fear also rushes all through them.

When Crug sees his wife, Ni'na, sitting at the rear of the cave, he comes over to her, stops and looks down into her face. "Gather things. We leave," he said.

Ni'na looks up at him with surprise. "Leave?"

"Crug leader of clan. We go south to old place."

"What happened?" she asked.

"Crug not follow Dearth. Men die. Dearth not good leader."

When Ursa hears that Crug is claiming to be the new clan leader, she fears that Dearth has also died and rushes over to confront Crug. "Dearth dead?" she asked, with tears welling up in her eyes.

Crug looks at her and shakes his head. "Dearth not dead. Dearth lead weak men. Crug lead strong men."

After Roosa hears that Dearth is alive but there have been other men that died, her worse fears come to the surface and she hurries over to Crug. "Who die" she asked, with tears already streaming down her face.

Crug stops gathering up his things and looks at her. "Nagar killed by great beast." He then looks over at Kuma and then Sora. "Brother Brant killed. Graun killed, too."

Kuma and Sora begin crying, but Crug just looks at them. "Gather things and come," he said. "We go back south where we came."

After they cry a while, Sora and Kuma begin gathering up their belongings. They are in shock and hardly know what they are doing. Finally, Roosa comes back over to Crug. "Will Crug burry dead?"

He looks at her with anger still in his eyes. "Dearth leader. He bury dead. Not clan of Crug."

It only takes Crug and those that are going with him a short time to gather their things, and before Dearth and the men with him returns, they leave. Those that leave with Crug are: Crug's wife, Ni'na; Bogg and his wife, Trusa; Durock and his wife, Tomah; Kuma, Sora and Garr's widow, Soma.

The women that have just lost their husbands and are leaving with Crug, and all are still crying bitter tears. Before they get a mile from the cave, they stop. Crug sees them stop and turns around. "Why stop?" he asked.

Kuma looks at him. "We want to see husbands put in ground."

This makes Crug angry, but he knows if he presses them too much, they may not go with him. He looks over to his wife, Ni'na. She nods and he knows he should let them go back and see their husbands buried.

"We wait here," he said. "Go back and see your men then come back. We wait."

Kuma and Sora nod, turn around and begin walking back to the cave.

Crug makes camp there and waits until the afternoon of the next day. He is about ready to break camp and leave when he sees the two women coming. They then all head south. If they only knew what awaited them there, however, they would have never gone.

Chapter 37

Tragedy Strikes

A few weeks after the clan splits, Ock learns that his wife, Ee'ga is pregnant. It is good news and the news causes everyone's spirits to rise. The departure of those that left with Crug was a shock and it upset every person that stayed. But now that a new member will be added to the clan there is joy once again.

Little Mulda is now five years old and Ulda has not been able to become pregnant again. She is happy, however, and feels blessed to have Mulda. Durr, too, loves Mulda and is proud that he is a father.

Then, just a few months later, tragedy is about to strike the clan once again. It is the beginning of winter and the herds of animals are moving south. Ock and Dearth spotted a small herd of mammoths about five miles north when they were scouting yesterday afternoon. Dearth decides they should go after them early the next day.

The hunting party makes an early start the next morning at sunrise. After they eat a small meal of bison meat, they grab their spears and head out in search of the mammoths. It is a much smaller hunting party now since Crug is gone and the three men were killed several months back. Augg is now crippled so he can no longer go on hunts. This will make it more difficult to bring down a mammoth, but the clan needs the meat to sustain them through the long cold winter. Otherwise they will have to kill several smaller animals.

In the hunting party is Dearth, Ock, Gogg, Durr and Mooth. Mooth has grown a lot in statue and in hunting skills since the mammoth killed the three men last spring. Hunting the "great beast" is still very dangerous, however, and with a much smaller hunting party it only compounds the danger.

As they approach the spot where Ock and Gogg spotted the mammoth herd the day before, they see that the herd has not moved more than a hundred yards from where they were feeding yesterday. The herd of eight animals is in a grove of small trees near a stream. The men see that most are young females with only one mature cow with a yearling calf. They decide they will try and take one of the young females.

Dearth motions for the men to get down and crawl on their hands and knees until they can reach the edge of the grove of trees. They will then get on both sides of the grove and close in on one of the animals. Once they are close enough, Dearth will pick out the one he wants and throw his spear. As soon as the spear strikes the animal, the others will launch their spears at the same mammoth.

The men stay downwind until they reach the small trees. Dearth looks over at Mooth, Durr and Gogg and motions for them to stay, while he and Ock go to the other side of the grove and sneak up on one of the feeding mammoths.

Everything goes great and soon Dearth and Ock are in position. Just a few yards away is a nice sized, young female cow and Dearth looks at Ock. The two hunters rise to their feet, pull back their first spear and pick out a spot on the mammoth's left ribcage. Then with all their might, they throw the spears, which sail to their mark and sink deep into the mammoth's side.

When they strike, she raises her ears and trunk in alarm and lets out an ear-piercing trumpet. This immediately alarms the rest of the herd. Instantly, the entire herd has their ears flared and their trunks and tails raised, trying to get the scent of whatever has attacked them.

Durr, Mooth and Gogg are now standing on their feet and as the wounded mammoth spins around in confusion, they throw their spears and hit it in the right side. When the spears hit her, she lets out another trumpeting scream and takes off crashing through the bushes and small trees, trying to escape. The big cow with her calf, however, has just gotten the scent of the three men nearest her and turns toward them.

Mooth and Gogg see that she is angry and probably thinks her calf is in danger. Before they can react, she lowers her head and rushes toward them in a charge. The men don't have much time to think. They hurriedly lift their spears and draw them back. If they run, the big cow can easily outrun them and crush them to death. They must stand their ground and hope her charge is a bluff.

A second later, they realize she is not bluffing and they throw all three spears, which strike her in the left shoulder and chest. This does not slow her down but seems to enrage her all the more. Durr is the closest and she sets her sights on him. Mooth and Gogg leap into the bushes because there is little else they can do.

Dearth and Ock see what is happening through the grove of trees and take off running toward the enraged animal. Each has one more spear apiece, which they clutch in their hands as they are running to save their clan member. When they come around the grove of trees, they are just in time to see the mad mammoth knock Durr to the ground. She then uses her head as a battering ram to drive him into the earth. It is not a pretty sight and Durr's screams can be heard as she crushes the life from him.

Dearth and Ock reach the scene in seconds and throw their spears, which causes the cow to break off her attack. It is far too late for Durr, however. As the cow runs off to catch up to the herd, the men look to see Durr lying still, his body twisted and broken.

Mooth and Gogg come from the bushes and join Dearth and Ock. Durr is dead and there is nothing anyone can do. This will kill his wife, Ulda. They will take the body back and bury it, but they can't take away the sadness they feel or the terrible grief that Ulda is about to experience.

Chapter 38

The Shock

When the men return from a hunt, the wives almost always meet them at the cave entrance. They usually hear them talking long before they arrive, but not today. Their silence alone tells the wives in advance that something is wrong when they start coming inside the cave.

When Dearth enters, the women look up and see he has a somber face. Ursa is the first to jump to her feet and come toward him. Ulda looks over at Ee'ga and they both run to meet their husbands. Behind Dearth, Ock walks in and Ee'ga runs to his side smiling but Ock does not smile back. Behind Ock is Mooth and Ulda stands there waiting for Durr to step through the entrance but he doesn't.

Dearth and the men with him can see the fear in Ulda's eyes, as she runs up to Dearth. "Where Durr?"

Dearth shakes his head. "Great beast attack and Durr not live."

Ulda begins shaking her head in disbelief. "Durr not dead! Husband cannot be dead! Durr outside playing trick," she said, trying to crack a smile. "Tell him to come inside."

Dearth shakes his head again and Ulda looks at the faces of Gogg and Ock and sees their sadness, too. She knows it is true, yet she feels as though everything at this moment is a dream, no a nightmare, and she wants to wake up and see her husband come through the entrance as he has hundreds of times before.

Dearth looks at Ursa and then over at Ulda. Ersa goes over to Ulda and puts her hand on her shoulder to comfort her.

"We bury Durr," Dearth said. "Outside by trail."

"Durr is in ground?" Ulda said, still unbelieving.

"Body crushed. Not good for Ulda to see."

"Take me to husband," she said, as tears began running down her cheeks.

When Augg hears what has happened, he calls Mulda over to his side and holds her. She is only five and she doesn't understand what has happened. She cannot comprehend the death of a human. She knows animals die but people are different. Just this morning her daddy was alive and hugged her goodbye. Now he is gone and will never hug Mulda again.

Braum is now seven and he understands it a little better, but he, too, has never had to deal with the loss of a clan member since he could remember. He comes over to Augg's side and stands by Mulda. "Mulda no cry," he said, putting his hand on her shoulder.

Mulda, however, cannot hold back the tears, especially when she sees her mother crying.

Dearth and Ock, along with the rest of the clan, follow Ulda outside into the cold to where Durr is buried.

Ulda does not have on any warm clothes, and Ursa runs and gets a heavy bison robe to cover her. Running to catch up, Ursa throws it over her shoulders and walks beside the grieving widow.

It is just a short distance from the cave entrance and Dearth steps up beside the fresh grave and stops.

When Ulda sees the grave, deep sorrow comes over her and she falls down on the grave on her knees, sobbing bitterly. "Why Durr die?" she cries, and everyone can feel her grief.

Ulda then looks up to the sky and begins to wail with moans of sadness as she remembers her husband. Then, falling on her face, she grasps the dirt in both hands and clutches it. The sight of her touches all of those there and the woman the most. They know it could have been their husband in the grave and it could be their sorrow she is enduring.

Finally, Ursa looks over at Ee'ga and they step up beside Ulda and help her to her feet. As they start walking away, Ulda turns and looks back at the grave. She then breaks away from them and again falls on the grave, crying for her husband.

When Dearth sees her great sorrow, he and Ock walk over and help her to her feet and escort her away. She again looks back and wants to run to the grave but the men hold onto her and take her to the cave.

When Ulda comes into the cave, Mulda sees her mother's face and runs to her. "Where Daddy?" she asked.

Ulda looks down into Mulda's sad eyes, does not answer but walks to the rear of the cave, sits down and looks as if she is in shock. Ursa and Roosa go and sit beside her, but there is little they can do to take away her grief. From this day forward Ulda will never be the same.

Chapter 39

Ulda's Condition

After the death of Durr, Ulda gives up on life. She does not eat right; she hardly sleeps and the other women must care for Mulda. The weeks soon turn into months and she does not get any better.

Then, one day as the men return from a hunt, she sees them come in and runs to meet Dearth. She is smiling for the first time since Durr was killed and for a moment, everyone thinks she might be getting better. But as she stands there, she watches the men come in and then looks over at Dearth. "Where Durr?" she asked, as if she had no recollection of her husband's death.

Dearth is taken aback by her question as are those listening. He doesn't answer but looks at Ursa who has just walked up to greet him.

Ursa comes over and puts her arm around Ulda. "Durr gone away on long hunt. He be back tomorrow."

This seems to comfort Ulda, she smiles and looks up into Ersa's eye. "Durr be back tomorrow?"

Ursa nods. "Durr be back tomorrow."

This happens every time the men go on a hunt and return. She is reliving the day her husband died. In her tormented mind she believes if she can go back to the day he died and the men return, perhaps they will tell her he is really alive or that he will walk in like he did so many times before. Her mind cannot handle the thought that he is never returning.

This goes on for over two months, and then she begins acting as though she is pregnant with the baby that died. One moment she will talk about having a baby and the next moment the child is alive and she is caring for him. Often, she will carry a parcel of folded skin in her arms and treat it as if it were a baby. She will sing to it and rock it to sleep. Her troubled mind is going back to the days her son, Drock, was alive that short week that he lived.

There is nothing anyone can do and they see that her health is going downhill. She has lost so much weight because she will not eat. Sometimes she does not even drink water for two or three days at a time.

After several months of going through this, she falls ill. No one knows if it is a sickness or if her body is just worn out from what she has put it through. She cannot even walk and lies on a pallet made of bison hides. The women try to get her to eat but she refuses. Mulda has just turned six and Mulda often tries talking to her. Ulda will just smile but everyone can see that she does not even recognize her own daughter.

After three weeks of being bedfast, Ulda dies in her sleep. It is heartbreaking for everyone but even more so for Mulda, for she is now an orphan.

Chapter 40

Gogg's Great Trial

One dies, one is born. That is the way life goes. Just a few weeks after Ulda's death, Gogg learns that Mursa is pregnant. Both are very happy and the news seems to cheer up nearly everyone. Mulda has come to grips with her mother's death. She had seen the sorrow Ulda had gone through for months before her death. Ursa explained that she is not suffering any longer and is better off than she was. This seems to comfort Mulda and with the other women caring for her, she is happier than she has been for a long time.

The months go by and Mursa is looking forward to the birth of her first child. Gogg also could not be more pleased and he is looking forward to fatherhood. He, of course, wants the baby to be a boy, so he can teach him how to hunt.

The day arrives that Mursa starts having labor pains but it is nearly a month too early. Fear suddenly grips her heart, but the women try to comfort her saying that the baby could still be born healthy.

The women get busy helping her prepare for the baby that's coming. Roosa is still acting as midwife as always and Ursa is also there to help, as well as to learn the how Roosa assists the mother during a birth.

The birthing rocks come in handy once again and after the pains get close together, she squats down between them.

Her labor lasts for several long hours and the baby has not yet been born.

Gogg has just gone outside with the other men, is waiting for the baby to be born and for one of the women to come and tell him.

Inside the cave, Mursa's contractions are getting harder and closer together.

"See head," Roosa said. "Push hard!"

Mursa waits for the next pain and with a final contraction she pushes as hard as she can and Roosa takes the infant in her hands. Roosa then turns around and puts the infant on a soft deerskin that has been placed on a rock behind her. But when she looks at the baby, she sees that it is not moving, its body is limp and it's not breathing. Grabbing the deerskin, she begins rubbing the baby all over, trying to get it to take its first breath. She then holds it up and blows into its mouth but there is no use, the baby is stillborn.

Mursa is watching and her heart is sinking by the moment. She keeps hoping the baby will take a breath and cry out. But then Roosa lays the baby's body down on the deerskin and covers it, looks over at Mursa and Ursa, and shakes her head. "Baby born dead. Not live."

Tears begin flowing down Mursa's cheeks. She saw that it was a boy and knows Gogg will be heartbroken when he learns he has lost a son.

Ursa goes outside to find him. Upon coming out of the cave, she sees him standing a short distance away talking with Ock, Dearth and Mooth. When Gogg sees her coming, he smiles and comes over to meet her. "Is baby here?"

Ursa does not answer right away but has sadness in her eyes. Gogg can tell she does not have good news. "What wrong?" Gogg asked.

"Baby born too early. Baby not live."

Gogg then thinks of his wife. "Mursa good?"

Ursa nods. "Musa good but sad."

Gogg says no more but hurries to Mursa's side.

When he comes near, she looks up from her pallet and starts crying. Gogg kneels down at her side. "No cry. Mursa have more babies, many babies."

Mursa tries to be brave and smiles through her tears trying to comfort herself, as well as Gogg. "Mursa have another son for husband."

When Gogg hears that it was a son that he lost, his heart aches but he knows he needs to not say anything. Mursa needs him more than ever now and he can't show his disappointment for her sake.

Three days pass and Mursa is still grieving over losing the baby, but women have lost babies before and gotten over it. It's the way things are for Neanderthals. Everyone believes everything will be fine given enough time. On the fourth morning, however, Gogg awakens beside Mursa and finds that she is burning up with fever. She does not know what is wrong and even if she did, there is nothing they can do about a uterus infection. She will either live or die.

For four days and nights, Mursa lies sick, growing weaker by the hour. Finally, her body can take no more and her organs begin shutting down. Gogg is kneeling beside her, holding her hand as she struggles to get her breath. Looking up into his sad eyes, she smiles. "Gogg good husband. Mursa sorry not strong woman. Sorry could not give Gogg son."

Gogg shakes his head. "Mursa good woman."

Mursa smiles again and closes her eyes, and then lets her last breath leave her body. She is gone and Gogg has never felt so alone. He lowers her hand down onto her breasts and gets up. When he stands, the others look over and know that Mursa has died and they each feel some of his sorrow. Gogg then walks outside into the cool air and goes off by himself so no one can see him cry.

Chapter 41

Ock's and Ee'ga's Baby

The last nine months have been rocky to say the least. It seems one tragedy after another has struck the clan. Just the past month, Roosa has started using a walking stick. Arthritis has settled in her hips and it is much more difficult for her to get around. Many of the clan members believe there is indeed a curse on them because of all the trouble and heartache they have endured. Ock's and Ee'ga's baby is due any day now and there is hope that things will finally turn around.

It is late morning when Ee'ga goes into labor. The men have just returned from a short hunt not far from the cave. When Ock learns that his wife is having the baby, he is overjoyed but worried at the same time. So many infants have been stillborn or died right after being born the last few years. Others have been miscarriages. This is running through Ock's mind and also through Ee'ga's. Roosa is there to help deliver the baby and tries to calm Ee'ga's fears.

It is a rather easy birth and a little five-pound baby girl comes into the world before nightfall. She appears to be very healthy and Ee'ga names her Troosa after Roosa, who has been the midwife of so many women the last several years.

Ock and Ee'ga are filled with joy as Ee'ga holds the baby to her breast and she nurses for the first time. She is so tiny but she already has a shock of thick, dark brown hair. She seems to enjoy her first meal and quickly goes to sleep afterwards.

As the days pass, however, she does not seem to gain any weight. In fact, she seems to lose some. Roosa assures Ee'ga that this is normal for many babies and she should start to gain weight soon. The days soon turn into weeks but Troosa does not grow as she should. She gains some weight but not nearly enough. She also cries all the time, as if she is hungry. It finally becomes apparent that the milk she is getting from her mother is not sufficient. It does not agree with her for some reason.

Ee'ga is beside herself with worry and so is Ock. There is nothing anyone can do, however. Ock even thought of trying to kill a female bison that has a calf and getting some milk from her. It would be possible but a dead bison would only give a small amount then the baby would be without any more, so it is hopeless.

By the third month, everyone knows the baby is losing the battle to stay alive. Little Troosa is nothing but skin and bones. Ee'ga carries the baby around all day and much of the night, trying get her to eat and to stop her from crying. Then one night they both fall asleep as Ee'ga is lying down holding her. The following morning, Ee'ga awakens and finds that little Troosa died sometime during the night.

Ee'ga is beside herself with grief. Roosa tries to comfort her saying these things sometimes happen and there is nothing anyone can do about them. Troosa growing up was just not meant to be.

Ock says little because he doesn't know what to say. His heart, too, is broken. A month after the baby died Ee'ga is sitting in the cave all alone crying. Everyone else has gone outside into the fresh air. Ee'ga does not feel like going out and being with the others. Her heart is just too heavy. In her mind, she keeps seeing the baby from the moment she was born to all the times she nursed her and laid her down to sleep. She can see Troosa in her mind growing up and becoming a woman. Each time she sees a new image of what was or what could have been, the tears start flowing down her cheeks.

Her grief is wearing on Ock and he has grief of his own. He must say something and, in his heart, he asks the Great Spirit to give him the words he needs to take away Ee'ga's sorrow.

Going over to where Ee'ga is sitting, Ock stops and stands beside her. Ee'ga looks up with tears in her eyes and Ock feels her sorrow. "Why Ee'ga still cry?" he asked.

"Still miss, Troosa."

"Troosa with Great Spirit now. Great Spirit take good care of baby Troosa. She not hungry. She not cold. She not cry no more. Troosa happy with Great Spirit."

Ee'ga takes the back of her hands and wipes the tears from her red swollen eyes. She then nods. "Troosa with Great Spirit. He take good care of her. Me not worry about baby no more." Ee'ga then looks into Ock's eyes and smiles.

That is the first smile he has seen since when she knew the baby was sick. Ock is shocked. That one sentence has taken away all of her sorrow. He then knows the Great Spirit must have given him the words just as he had asked.

Chapter 42

The Strangers

About a hundred miles to the south, Crug and his small clan have settled in their old cave. Two years have passed without incident. Meat isn't abundant as it was when the clan was larger, but they are managing. Everything has been going fairly well up to this time, but nothing stays the same forever.

It is nearing autumn and Crug, along with his brother Bogg, and clan member Durock, are hunting bison just a few miles south of their cave, when they see a small band of people coming their way. Durock is the first to spot them and he turns to Crug. "People come," he said, pointing with his spear.

Crug looks over at him and then to where he is pointing. It looks to be several Neanderthal women and children along with a man. The man seems to be injured and is slightly stooped over. They are about three hundred yards away and coming right toward them.

"We go see," Crug said, and the three men begin walking to meet them.

When they come near, the women appear to be frightened, as do the children who are clinging to their mother's clothing. The man accompanying them is a young man, perhaps in his mid-twenties. He is rather short but robust with a long, bushy beard, which matches his curly brown hair. He is holding his left arm in his right hand as the two groups meet. Crug stops a few feet away and the man steps forward, looks up into Crug's face and grimaces from apparent pain.

"What happened?" Crug asked.

The women hold their children close to them in fear, not knowing if Crug's hunting party is friendly or not.

"Strange men attack hunting party," the man said.

"Why men attack?" Crug asked.

"Strange men not Neanderthal men. Tall and thin. Have weapons never seen. Weapons throw tiny spear like lightening. Spear kill all men in hunting party. I run fast but tiny spear hit my shoulder. I run to cave — take women and children far away."

His story sounds unbelievable to Crug and his men.

Crug walks around to the side of the man and turns him slightly so he can see the wound. He has it covered with a strip of bison hide and Crug lifts it so he can see. It is a deep wound and does look like a tiny spear has struck him.

"Where strange men come from?" Durock ask, stepping forward to look at the wound himself.

"Not know. Must come from south."

Crug thinks for a moment then looks around at the women and children, then back at the man. "Come with Crug. Women and children be safe."

The man nods. "I Gomar," he said, looking at Crug. "You leader?"

Crug nods and turns to the men with him. "That Durock," he said, looking at him as Durock nods. Then looking at Bogg he adds, "That Bogg." Bogg also nods and they all begin walking back to Crug's cave.

When they arrive at the cave, the women there are more than surprised to see five women and six children come in with their Crug and his small hunting party. Then they see the injured man come in. They do not know what to think except there must have been trouble.

Crug's wife, Ni'na, comes up to him. "Where people come from?"

"Found them walking from south. Man say strange men attack hunting party and kill all men. He run to cave, take women and children away."

Ni'na is very concerned. "Strange men?"

"Man say tall men with little spears that go like lightening, kill all hunting party and hit him when he run away."

"Who strange men? Where come from?" Ni'na asked.

"Not know," he answered, as he watched the women and children going to the rear of the cave and sitting down. "People hungry. Feed them."

Ni'na looks at him and whispers, "Strange men will come to find man. Come here and kill us."

"Strange men not kill Crug. Crug kill strange men," he said, with assurance.

Ni'na does not have the same confidence as her husband. She is very afraid, as are the other women. No one knows who these strange men are or where they come from. Only time will tell if her fears are justified.

Chapter 43

The Final Chapter

Unknown to Crug, the strange men have a village not far away. They are a new race of humans that will later be known as Cro-Magnons. They are more advanced than Neanderthals and are on a mission to eradicate every clan of Neanderthals they can find. They kill all the men and old women. They take the young women as sex slaves and either kill or enslave the children. In their eyes, the Neanderthals are subhuman and are to be destroyed wherever they are found.

The Cro-Magnons have also invented the bow and arrow and they use them very efficiently. The crude spears the Neanderthals use are not nearly as deadly as the arrows, which can be shot at a much greater distance, long before a Neanderthal man can get close enough to throw his spear.

Besides the bow and arrow, the Cro-Magnons have learned to make metal, which they use on their arrow tips and on their hunting spears, and even as shields. They also weave clothing, although they do use animal skins much the same way as Neanderthals do.

The Cro-Magnons have been coming north for many years. On their way, they have been systematically wiping out any Neanderthals they find. Now they are but two days walk from Crug's clan and today a hunting party of Cro-Magnons will find them.

It has been nearly a month since Crug came across the injured man and his clan. No tall strange men have come and most of their fear has subsided. Crug thinks the man was mistaken and the men that attacked the man's hunting party were just a bad group of Neanderthals. As for the tiny arrows, he doesn't know what to think. Perhaps they did have a new weapon.

The following week, a hunting party of a dozen Cro-Magnon men is led by a man called Eric. Eric is tall with light brown hair. He wears a leather helmet with bison horns on it. He carries a bow that can kill a bison or a man at a hundred yards if he can hit them. At thirty-yards he is a dead shot with the weapon. His men are likewise proficient with a bow and with a spear. Both their spears and their arrows are tipped with razor sharp metal, which is bronze.

As Eric and his men come to the top of a small hill, one of his men looks below and sees something move. A second later, the man sees a woman step out from behind a bush. The man looks toward Eric who is out front. "There's a woman down below," he said.

The men stop and look back at him. He is pointing down the hill and they all look to see Soma beside a stream filling a water bag.

Eric motions for the men to stay low and they begin sneaking down the hill toward her. When they get within a few yards, Eric sees that she is certainly a Neanderthal and he looks at the man nearest him and nods. The man stands to his feet, pulls back his bow and releases his arrow. It flies right toward Soma and sinks deep into her chest. She looks up and sees the men rushing towards her as she drops the bag of water and falls to the ground.

Soma can feel her life slipping away as she lies there. A moment later, she sees the men step up beside her and look down. They are all around her and are smiling as they watch her die. One of the men bends over and speaks, "Many men in clan?" Eric asked.

Soma nods her head, hoping they might be afraid to attack her people if they know there are many men there to fight.

"Woman lie," Eric said.

"All Neanderthals lie," another man said.

"Let's go see how many there are," Eric said, looking over at the man that shot Soma.

The man nods, reaches down, takes hold the arrow shaft and jerks it from Soma's chest. She tries to scream but only groans. She then passes out from the pain. She will never awaken, however, for she has already lost too much blood. Her lungs are filling with blood and a moment later, she is gone.

Eric and his men then follow the path Soma took to come to the stream. A few minutes later, they see the cave up ahead. It is mid-morning and the men of Crug's clan are out on a hunt. The only ones left are the women.

Eric and those with him stop a few yards from the cave entrance and watch. After several minutes it seems apparent that there are no Neanderthal men there. They have seen a couple of women come outside then return to the cave. They have heard women's voices from inside the cave but no voices of men.

Eric looks at his men and motions for them to go to the cave. The men nod, clutch their bows and spears as they rush toward the entrance of the cave. When they enter, they have their bows drawn and their spears raised.

Inside the cave, the children are running around playing. Most of women are sitting near the back of the cave talking when Eric and his men bust through the entrance. Upon seeing them, the women turn around and scream.

They have never seen such men before, neither have they seen a bow and arrow, which is pointed right at them.

When the children see the strange men enter the cave, they run to their mothers and cling to them for protection.

When Eric steps inside, he looks the women over as they huddle together in fear. Most of Crug's original female clan members are old and already have much grey hair. But some of the new female clan members are fairly younger.

When he sees Kuma, he goes over, takes her by the arm and pulls her to her feet. "This one will be good slave," he said, shoving her toward the men.

One of the men grabs her by the arm and smiles.

Eric then sees Sora. She is just a little older than Kuma and he grabs her and gives her to another man. The newer women of the clan are a few feet away from the others and Eric points to them and the children, then motions for the men to go take them.

While the men are grabbing the woman of their choice, the women begin screaming and the children start crying. The men only laugh as they begin tearing the women's clothing off to see what they look like. They are pleased at what they see and start ravishing them as the children stand there crying and watching.

Eric then steps back and looks at the other women, who are Ni'na, Trusa and Tomah. After looking them over, he doesn't see one young enough to suit his purposes. Turning around, he walks away and calls over to his men, "Take care of the old women."

They stop assaulting the younger women, pick up their bows and come over near the older women. Raising their weapons, they pull back their bowstrings, point the arrows at Ni'na, Trusa and Tomah and then shoot. When the three arrows are released, each strike one of the women in the upper chest and they all slump to the cave floor.

It takes them a moment to die, and as their life is draining from their bodies, they look around at all those in the cave. Slowly their eyes flicker, then close, and they are gone.

Kuma and Sora begin screaming but the men only laugh. Eric then comes over to Kuma as the other men go back to raping the others. "When men return from hunt?" he asked.

Kuma is terrified and looks into Eric cold eyes. Shaking her head, she answers, "Not know."

Eric looks angry as he leans down and looks into her frightened eyes. "When men leave?"

Kuma looks over at Sora, as if to ask what she should say, but this makes Eric angry. He then grabs her chin in his hand and jerks her head back so she is facing him. "Answer me!" he snapped. "When did your men leave?"

Kuma tries to speak but Eric's hand is muffling her speech, so she mumbles and Eric cannot understand her. He removes his hand and Kuma repeats what she tried to say, "Men leave early this morning."

"How many men?" Eric asked again.

Kuma looks around at all the men that have stopped assaulting the women to watch what their leader is doing. She knows what will happen to the men in her clan if she answers, but she has no choice.

Eric turns to her with anger all over his face then turns and points to the dead woman on the cave floor. "You want to die with other women? How many men?"

Kuma holds up her right hand and shows Eric four fingers.

He turns to his men. "There's only four of them. That is if this Neanderthal can count that high."

The men laugh and go back to raping the women.

Eric smiles. "We will just wait until they return and give them a warm greeting," he said, laughing and pushing Kuma to the man he had given her to.

"A greeting they will remember for the rest of their lives, which will be very short," said the man, grabbing Kuma.

Eric stands guard while the men enjoy the women. When they are finished, the men go over and have a seat to wait. The women are crying as they gather up their clothing and put them back on. The children are still crying and run to their mothers for comfort.

While Eric and his men are waiting, Eric makes Kuma and Sora roast them some bison meat. About two hours later, Eric and his men hear Crug and the three men with him talking. Eric looks at his men, then over at Kuma and Sora. Two men rush over and cover their mouths so that they can't warn the approaching men.

Eric has his men standing in the center of the cave with their bows drawn and ready as the unsuspecting men come inside. When Crug and Gomar step through the entrance of the cave, they are shocked to look up and see Eric and his men standing there. Their eyes are full of fear but they don't have time to react or even say a word. All they see is an arrow come from a weapon that Crug has never seen and Gomar has only seen once. A split-second later, the men feel the metal tipped arrows sink deep in their chests. Instantly they drop to the cave floor and lie there bleeding to death.

Durock and Bogg are right behind Crug and Gomar and are carrying the hindquarters of a wild boar when they, too, are struck by arrows. The men drop to the cave floor beside the two dying men along with the meat they are carrying and begin moving trying to get back to their feet. When they look up at the strange men, they see that they have nocked another arrow and a second later they feel the bronze tipped heads hit them again. This time they only have a few seconds as they see the strange men smile, then everything goes black.

Eric and his men never realize that Gomar was the one they wounded a while back. They just assumed he died and Crug's clan always had four adult men.

Kuma and Sora see their men slaughtered and are horrified. They try to scream but the men still have their hands over their mouth. As soon as the men are dead, the Cro-Magnons take their hands away and the women fall to the cave floor weeping.

After Eric and his men retrieve their arrows from the bodies of the dead men, they take the women and children and leave. The men will force the women to serve them by threatening the children with death or beatings. Kuma and Sora will live out the rest of their days as slaves. While they are still relatively young, they will also be used for the men's enjoyment.

Eric will continue searching for more Neanderthals, so he can exterminate them. He and his kind feel Neanderthals are subhuman and need to be eradicated from the earth. They believe there isn't enough game for both races, nor is there enough room for them to coexist. They believe this because they want to. It is an excuse to murder and enslave another race.

It will be two years, however, before they move far enough north to find Dearth's clan, but find them they will. Now you know the rest of the story.

Back at Dearth's cave, he has no idea there is a Cro-Magnon settlement that is a hundred miles south or that they have killed Crug and most of his clan. He could not even imagine that there is a new race of humans led by a thirty-year-old man named Eric, or that Eric and his men are the advance force that are searching for and destroying the Neanderthal people. He could not fathom that someone would think that Neanderthals are not human. Neither could he understand that the Cro-Magnons justify the slaughter of his people by claiming the Neanderthals are taking the animals the Cro-Magnons need for food. To the Cro-Magnons to kill a Neanderthal is just good sport and they enjoy it. To the Cro-Magnons, that is all the excuse they need.

It will be two years before Eric settles close enough to Dearth's clan to find them, but it is just a matter of time before they do. The Cro-Magnon village will only be two days walk from Dearth's people. When they arrive, the Neanderthals will have no chance of defeating the more advanced race of human.

At Dearth's cave, he and the other men are getting ready to go on a hunt. Small herds of mammoths have been spotted close by and the men are anxious to make a kill. Their meat supply is getting low and they have no other choice than to face the huge and dangerous animals.

Dearth, along with Ock, Gogg and Mooth pick up their spears then turn to leave. Dearth's wife, Ersa, hurries over and hugs him good-bye. Ee'na, likewise, comes over to Ock, hugs him and wishes him good luck on the hunt. The women never know if this will be the last time they shall ever see their husbands.

This is where the prequel ends and the first book of *The Mammoth Slayers* begins. Thank you.

Epilogue

This ends the prequel to the Mammoth Slayers. It was not easy writing a prequel, as I had to go back and tell how the people in the series came to be and all that led up to the first story. I did my best to make the saga of the Mammoth Slayers interesting, so I hope you have enjoyed reading it.

Although it was a lot of work writing the stories and I spent many long hours at the laptop writing them, it was enjoyable. We can never know all the trials and tribulations that these primitive people went through, we can guess there were many. With no doctors or medicine, many died of what would be simple cures today. I'm also sure that infant mortality was high.

It was a harsh life but the only one they knew and just like us, they had hopes and dreams. They loved and were loved. They had conflicts and I'm sure much sorrow and grief as well. I tried to write the story with as much realism as possible, yet much of it conjecture because no one knows what took place; we can only guess by what scientists have found so far. I also used my imagination to try to bring the characters to life. I believe I did, although some may disagree.

Many of the emotions the characters felt, I myself have experienced, especially the sorrow and grief of losing loved ones. Therefore, as I was writing and editing the books, I often shed tears and sometimes I had to stop because I could not see the computer screen because of them. I have had readers tell me when they reviewed the books they likewise shed tears as they became attached to the people in the story and felt sorrow when they died. I try to write from my heart because if I don't feel something, how can my readers feel it? Thank you.

About the Author

Kenneth Edward Barnes has been called, *"A modern day Mark Twain"* by a local newspaper reporter. *"He shows a Twain sense of humor in conversation and in his writing. He writes in the 'down to earth' style that Twain used to capture the heart of America."*

He was born on April 4, 1951, along the banks of Little Pigeon Creek in the southern tip of Indiana, downstream from where Abraham Lincoln grew up. As a child, he loved fishing from the muddy banks of the creek and roaming in the nearby woods. He never missed an opportunity to be in the outdoors where he could see all of God's creation.

Ken is a nationally published writer, poet and the author of over one hundred books. Some of his most popular ones are: *The Mammoth Slayers; A Cabin in the Woods;*

Mysteries of the Bible; *Madam President*; *Life Along Little Pigeon Creek*; *Children's Stories II*; *The Golden Sparrow*; *Buddy and Rambo: The Orphaned Raccoons*; *Barnestorming the Outdoors*; *The Arkansas River Monster series, and Do Pets go to Heaven?* This could soon change, however, as he has recently written several others.

The author became a member of *Hoosier Outdoor Writers* in 1993, where he has won several awards from them in their annual writing contest. He has also been a guest speaker for the *Boy Scouts, Daughters of the American Revolution, Teachers Reading Counsel, Kiwanis Club*, and at several schools, libraries and churches.

Ken has been an outdoor columnist and contributing editor for several newspapers and magazines: *Ohio Valley Sportsman, Kentucky Woods and Waters, Southern Indiana Outdoors, Fur-Fish-Game, Wild Outdoor World, Mid-West Outdoors,* and a hard cover book titled *From the Field.* He has written for the *Boonville Standard, Perry County News, Newburgh Register and Chandler Post.* He has had poems published locally and nationally. One titled *The Stranger* went to missionaries around the world. The poem, *Princess,* was also published locally and nationally, and won honorable mention in a national contest. His best-loved poem is *Condemned* and has been published by the tens of thousands. Nearly every single poem he has written is in his book *Poems From My Heart.*

Ken has worked for an Evansville, Indiana, television station where he had outdoor news segments aired that he wrote, directed and edited. He also had film clips that were aired on the national television shows *Real TV* and *Animal Planet.* In addition, the author has several videos on YouTube. Some are of his radio and television interviews and some videos are of the animals he has raised or him reading some of his work.

Studying nature since childhood, he is a self-taught ornithologist and a conservationist. In 2009, he became founder and president of the *Golden Sparrow Nature Society*, the name of which was chosen because of his first published book. Ken loves to share his knowledge and love of nature, and it has been said that he is a walking encyclopedia on birds and animals. Because of this, he recently published an e-book titled *Birds and Animals of Southern Indiana*. It has over 300 photos of birds and animals, most of which he photographed himself. He frequently updates it with new photos.

He has followed his dream of being a writer since 1978 and now lives in a cabin in the woods. Being an individualist, he cleared the land, dug a well by hand and built the house himself, which uses only solar electric. He even wrote a book titled *Solar Electric: How does that work?*

Comments on the author's work can be left on his Facebook page at: **Kenneth Edward Barnes**, or on **Twitter** at **Kenneth Edward Barne @BarneKenneth**. All of Ken's books can be seen on his **Author Page** at Amazon.

Other Books by Kenneth Edward Barnes in:
Paperback and E-book

1. A Biblical Mystery: Christians need to become a Jew: What does this mean?
2. A Cabin in the Woods
3. A Day Appointed
4. A House Divided: This is why Donald Trump won the election
5. A Rude Awakening
6. Abortion: Why all the controversy?
7. Barnestorming the Outdoors: Revised edition
8. Betrayed
9. Beyond the Grave: Is there life after death?
10. Bible Secrets Revealed
11. Buddy and Rambo: The Orphaned Raccoons
12. Children's Stories II
13. Christ: His Words, His Life
14. Christ: Who is He?
15. Christ's Second Coming: Is it near? How will we know?
16. Coincidences?
17. Death is his Name
18. Do Pets go to Heaven?

19. Evolution: The BIG Lie!
20. Faith: Is faith in God dying?
21. Flesh Wounds of the Mind
22. For the Love of God
23. For the Love of Nature: Four Stories About Birds and Animals
24. God's Holy Days
25. Gun Control: What's the Answer?
26. I'd Rather be Right than Politically Correct
27. Into the West
28. Jerusalem: City of peace?
29. Kenneth Edward Barnes: An autobiography
30. Kenny's Children's Stories
31. Life Along Little Pigeon Creek
32. Loneliness: How to deal with it
33. Madam President
34. Marriage, Infidelity, Divorce: What does the Bible say about it?
35. Mysteries of the Bible
36. Mystery of the Antichrist
37. Mystery of the Millennium
38. Odds and Ends
39. Plays for Children
40. Poems From My Heart
41. Ransom
42. Return of the Arkansas River Monster
43. Saving Wildlife
44. That's Bellabuggery: What in the world does that mean?
45. The Arkansas River Monster
46. The Arkansas River Monster: The complete series
47. The Black Widow
48. The Book of HUMOR
49. The Book of WISDOM (Words Instructing Spiritual Direction Of Man)
50. The Capture of the Arkansas River Monster
51. The Coming Invasion
52. The Creature of O'Minee
53. The Day that Time Stood Still

54. The Five Dimensions of Sex
55. The Golden Sparrow
56. The Last Arkansas River Monster
57. The Long Pond Road
58. The Invasion of the Dregs
59. The Mammoth Slayers
60. The Mammoth Slayers: Last Clan of Neanderthals
61. The Mammoth Slayers: The Last Neanderthal
62. The Mammoth Slayers: Rise of the Cro-Magnons
63. The Mammoth Slayers: The Prequel
64. The Ruby Ring and the Impossible Dream
65. The Unexplained
66. The War on Christians
67. The Words and Life of Jesus
68. Thou Shall Not Kill: What does God think about the killing of animals?
69. To Keep a Secret
70. What in the World is Wrong?
71. Why Does God Let Bad Things Happen?
72. Words to Live By

Books Available as E-books only

73. Is There a Devil? Is Satan Real?
74. The Thirteenth Disciple
75. The Two Witnesses
76. The Mammoth Slayers: Why the series was written
77. Birds and Animals of Southern Indiana
78. The Ancient Art of Falconry
79. Solar Electric: How does that work?
80. Instruction Manual for the WIFE (Wonderful Idea From Eden)
81. How to Care for your MAN (Mate's Animalistic Needs)
82. How to Raise your CHILD (Cute Huggable Innocent Little Darling)
83. INSTINCTS (Interesting Nature Secret Tendencies If Nature Could Teach Secrets)

Made in the USA
Las Vegas, NV
11 February 2021